Yule Tide

by

Brian Anderson

Yule Tide

Cover Art by *Tina Lynn Stout*

The Wild Rose Press, Inc.
PO Box 708
Adams Basin, NY 14410-0708
Visit us at www.thewildrosepress.com

Publishing History
First Edition, 2024
Trade Paperback ISBN 978-1-5092-5680-8
Digital ISBN 978-1-5092-5681-5

Published in the United States of America

Dedication

To my wife and daughters and all the wonderful
Christmases we have shared.

Chapter One

Dawn was breaking across the greasy December skies over the Northern California town of Yule Tide. Harold Angel blinked repeatedly, trying to scrape off some of the film that seemed to cover his eyes. He couldn't remember having fallen asleep; nor could he pinpoint the exact moment he had awakened. He'd simply opened his eyes and found himself at his desk dressed in the same clothes he'd donned the previous day.

Or…he thought it had been the previous day.

Sometime that same week anyway.

Angel swallowed hard. His tongue was too large for his mouth. He searched the top of his desk for something to drink, anything to cut the syrupy coating that lined his tongue. He found a Styrofoam coffee cup still filled with about two fingers of cold coffee. Next to this, lying on its side, he found the remains of a bottle of scotch, its cap gone, but with just enough liquid remaining for one swallow. Angel drained the bottle, spit loudly into the coffee cup, and turned to look out the window.

Streaks of yellow and orange from the rising sun fanned out to contend with the dark gray of the retreating night sky. Angel laughed. He knew that even in the full light of the coming day, the gray would emerge victorious. It was just that kind of place.

The color gray seemed to permeate every part of

Yule Tide, from the streets of the port city—which year-round were decked out in drooping holly and lusterless tinsel—to the souls of its inhabitants as they shuffled slowly about their daily duties, all, as if by decree, wearing toothy grins plastered on their faces. Even the castle on the hill, the focal point of the city, the great gingerbread mansion of the jolly, old elf himself, was clouded with a gray so pervasive and dispiriting that it left holiday visitors feeling lost and frightened, like blind children feeling their way across a busy intersection.

Angel turned from the window. He picked up the whiskey bottle, assured himself it was indeed empty, and finally tossed it into a metal wastebasket by the desk. The bottle landed with a loud clang, but as that sound died away, he became aware of another—the sound of shallow, labored breathing. As he swiveled his chair toward the sound, a low moan filled the room.

Curled up on the couch along the far wall of Angel's office, covered by a worn, brown corduroy overcoat, lay a small figure. Letting out another moan, the figure turned, and the overcoat fell to the floor.

Angel smiled.

He had to struggle to keep from laughing every time he looked at his little friend. Although Billy Goodman had lost his job at the toy factory many years before, he still insisted on wearing the multicolored uniform they had issued him the first day he reported for the job. The years had not been kind to either Billy or the uniform. Drink had bloated his elfin body, and as he lay asleep on Angel's couch, the buttons that fastened the dingy, rainbow-colored fabric across his midsection seemed ready to burst. One of his pointed shoes lay on the floor next to him. The other, still on his foot, sported a hole through which protruded Billy's great toe. Angel shook his head, unable to remember a single time in all the years that they had known each other that he had seen Billy in anything but these same clothes. And Angel had known Billy since the old days. Since before Kringle died. Since the days at the Pole.

Just as Angel rose from his chair to wake his friend from his slumber, the phone rang. The sleeping elf sprang to his feet and had the receiver in his hand before he even opened his eyes. Billy coughed, cleared his throat, coughed again, and in a high-pitched but quite professional and polished voice said, "Merry Christmas. Angel Investigations. May I help you?"

Angel waited as Billy listened to the caller, nodding his head from time to time as if in agreement. Finally, Billy said, "If it's that important, I'll see if he's in. It really is quite early you know."

Billy cupped a hand over the receiver, and opening his eyes for the first time, handed the phone to Angel. "Some dame, Harry."

Angel held on to the phone for some seconds before bringing it to his mouth. "This is Angel," he said at last. "How can I help you?"

The woman's voice was soft but with a lovely huskiness, like that of a blues singer lost in a ballad, or a good bourbon—smooth yet tingling with spent fire.

"Mr. Angel," the caller said, "I do apologize for calling so early in the morning, but you must understand that I'm desperate. I don't know where to turn. If you can't help me, I'm...I'm lost. I won't know what to do. I'll just...I'll..."

"Slow down. Slow down," Angel said. "I don't like to discuss things of a private nature over the phone. But we can talk about all of this in my office. Perhaps you can stop by here about…um, shall we say about ten o'clock. Will that be convenient, Miss…?"

"Ten o'clock? Ten o'clock will be fine, Mr. Angel. Oh, and it's Mrs., actually. Mrs. Deo."

"I'll see you at ten, Mrs. Deo."

Billy cocked an eyebrow as Angel hung up the phone. "What did she want?"

"I don't know yet," Angel answered. "I just hope this doesn't turn into another charity case. We haven't had a paying client in weeks."

"Months," Billy corrected.

"Just clean this place up, will you?" Angel said as he pulled a comb from his pocket and walked toward the office door.

By ten o'clock the office had been cleaned up, the trash taken out, the windows opened to clear out the lingering smell of booze and morning breath. Both Angel and Billy had done their best to make themselves presentable as well. Angel had actually succeeded.

Although a fallen angel, he'd retained the rugged good looks, the thick, dark hair and penetrating eyes that had made him stand out in the old days. And although the radiant, white robe of old was gone, Angel filled out his tailored pinstriped suit quite nicely. Billy had done what he could. He had run a comb through what little hair he had, but then covered his head with the tall, pointed cap that matched the rest of his uniform. When he went to the mirror to admire himself, his squinty smile so accentuated the deep wrinkles of his face that he looked like an over-plump, pink raisin in a harlequin outfit.

At three minutes after ten, the office door opened.

Their client was tall. That was the first thing Angel noticed. The next thing he noticed was the way she filled out the clinging, blue silk dress she wore. Curve followed curve perfectly as if she'd been sculpted by skilled hands. Luxuriant brown tresses tumbled about her sturdy shoulders. The lines of her strong back and full breasts flowed subtly down to her tiny waist, a waist so small even Billy's elfin hands might cup it in an embrace. Full, womanly hips flared then melded into long, athletic legs.

Angel found himself staring into her beautiful face. The light from the lamp by the office door cast a yellow halo upon her porcelain features, her enchanting green eyes, her nose, ever so slightly turned up, her rich, full mouth, and her smile. When she smiled, she presented a slight overbite of gleaming white teeth—small and sharp and inviting.

The click of the door as she closed it behind her snapped Angel from his reverie. He turned and found Billy's eyes fixed on their visitor in a kind of dreamy stupor. He was barely breathing.

Angel advanced, extending a hand to their lovely client. "Mrs. Deo," he said, "I'm Harold Angel. Over there is my friend and colleague Billy Goodman. Will you take a seat and please tell us how we can be of assistance to you?"

Mrs. Deo took her place in the leatherette easy chair that Angel kept in front of his desk for clients. Angel sat behind his broad desk, leaned back in his chair, and waited for his client to begin. Billy stood rooted in place, his gaze unyielding, now with an imbecilic leer on his face.

"I want you to find my husband, Mr. Angel," she

began. "He has been missing for five days. After he didn't come home from work, I immediately went to the police. They said that they couldn't help me until he had been missing for three days. When the three days passed, I went back to the police. They said that they would open a file and if they heard anything, they would let me know. Would it surprise you, Mr. Angel, to know that they have yet to hear anything?"

"No, Mrs. Deo, it would not," Angel said.

"I thought not," she continued. "I have heard it said that the police in this town could not find a missing person if he or she was surgically grafted to the police chief's ass."

Angel chuckled. "Now where did you hear something like that, Mrs. Deo?"

"I hope you will forgive such a coarse remark. I have spent much of the last two days waiting uselessly in the police station. I have found it difficult to remain myself having spent so much time among those who more often frequent the station house."

"Don't apologize, Mrs. Deo. It's quite all right, I assure you."

"I have concluded that I simply cannot rely solely on the police. The Company has promised to help, but I have my doubts that even they will be able to put much effort into discovering my husband's whereabouts. Not this close to Christmas. I know that, after the recent layoffs, they are dreadfully short staffed and even their security personnel are pitching in on the line trying to fill Christmas orders."

"Your husband works for the Company, then, Mrs. Deo?"

She waved her hand dismissively. "Everyone in this

town works for the Company," she said. "In one way or another."

Angel smiled. "I work for myself, Mrs. Deo."

Mrs. Deo sat silently for a moment, resting a quizzical gaze on Angel. "I came here," she said at last, "I came here in the hope that you would work for me, Mr. Angel."

He nodded and rose from behind his desk. There was a coffee maker in a corner of the office on top of a black metal filing cabinet. Billy had brewed a fresh pot before their client's arrival. Angel chose a cup from the stack and poured. He turned back to his client. "Coffee?"

She declined with a slight shake of her head.

Returning to his desk chair, Angel asked. "What does your husband do for the Company, Mrs. Deo?"

"My husband is Luther Deo, special administrative assistant to the Claus.

Angel nodded and let out a quiet whistle of appreciation.

"He's a man of great responsibility then," Angel said. "I'm surprised that his disappearance has not made the papers."

Mrs. Deo looked flattered. "The Company thought it best if the media were kept out of it, Mr. Angel. Aside from their conclusion that the media spotlight might harm our chances of finding out what happened to Luther, they do not want the public at large to interpret the disappearance of one of their top executives as something that will interfere with Christmas."

"Yeah," Angel said. "That would be a damn shame."

Angel and Mrs. Deo stared at each other for several seconds before Mrs. Deo asked, "You are not on the best of terms with the Company, then, Mr. Angel?"

"I have a simple relationship with the Company, Mrs. Deo. They have forgotten that I exist, and I have grown to appreciate that very much."

"You were with the Company in the past?"

"That's not something we need to discuss at this time. Perhaps you could tell me more about the circumstances of your husband's disappearance. Is it possible that he simply went somewhere without telling you?" Angel paused. "Men sometimes do that, you know."

"I do not believe that my husband simply left of his own accord. He is an important man with an important job to do. It is nearly Christmas and Christmas *is* what he spends the whole year working toward. He is the Claus's right-hand man. His disappearance is sorely felt by both the Company and the Claus himself. Luther would not abandon his post at a time like this. He understands what that would mean to the Company and to the public at large.

"Besides," she continued, "he would not leave me. Our relationship is such that it is inconceivable that he would, say, leave me for another woman. If that's what you are thinking, you can put that idea right out of your head."

Angel took a long, measured look at the woman who sat across from him. He put his fingertips together and leaned back in his chair. "Do you have any idea what happened to your husband?" he asked after a moment. "Have you had any ransom demands, for instance."

"No, none,"

"Does your husband have any enemies?"

"My husband is a man has spent the last few years ensuring that everyone's Christmas wishes are fulfilled.

No, I do not believe that he has any enemies."

Angel laughed, then took a long sip of his coffee. "I know more than you might suppose about the Company, Mrs. Deo," he said "Anyone who has managed to rise to your husband's position within the Company has made a few enemies. More than a few enemies."

"What is that supposed to mean?"

"It means that you have come to the right place for help, Mrs. Deo," Angel said, ignoring her puzzled expression. "Just a few more questions. Have you noticed anything peculiar since your husband's disappearance? Is there anything missing from your home? Does anyone seem to be following you?"

"I didn't want to mention it because I thought you might think it silly. Nothing is missing from our condo, but as I pulled out of the driveway this morning, I thought I saw a van. A blue van. I saw the same van as I crossed the street to your office just a few minutes ago. I told myself that it was probably just nerves. Do you really think…I mean is it possible that…"

"Don't worry about it, Mrs. Deo. As you say, it's probably just nerves. This has been a trying time for you. You just leave everything to me."

"You're very kind, Mr. Angel."

Mrs. Deo rose slowly, smoothing the wrinkles from her dress as she stood. Billy was still standing in the same place, continuing to stare, a little bubble of spit pulsating in one corner of his mouth.

Mrs. Deo offered Angel her hand. Angel rose and took her hand gently. "Just one more thing, Mrs. Deo. I'm sorry that I have to mention it. I will only be able to act in your interests in the legal sense if you put me on retainer. Shall we say a check for, oh, let's say a thousand dollars?"

Mrs. Deo smiled. "Of course, Mr. Angel."

She pulled her checkbook from her purse and in a small, tight hand filled out the amount and signed it. She handed it to Angel who, without looking at it, folded it and placed it in his breast pocket. "I've written my cell phone number on the check, Mr. Angel. Please keep me informed. I do so hope to have Luther home with me for the holidays."

"We will do our best, Mrs. Deo."

"Goodbye, then."

When his client had left, Angel returned to his chair. He pulled the check from his coat pocket and examined it closely. Eight tiny reindeer were drawing a heavily laden sleigh across the upper edge of the check. Beneath them, the name "Gloria Inexcelsis Deo" was written in calligraphic script.

Billy shook himself back into consciousness. He looked at Angel, then smiled and looked back at the closed office door. "My God," he said at last, sighing as if he had held his breath the whole time she'd been in the room with them. "My God, Boss. That was the most beautiful full-sized woman I have ever seen."

Angel smiled. "Careful, Billy. That's what kept you from getting that foreman job with the Company. Somebody's wife? What was her name? Felicia, or something?"

Billy's tiny body shook with laughter. "I can't help it," he said. "Women love me."

Angel nodded. "Well, it looks like we got work."

"Not just work," Billy said, his smile widening. "We got someone desperate enough to give us a thousand bucks. We ain't had a thousand bucks between us since I don't know when."

Angel refolded the check and put it back in his pocket.

"The thing is, Billy," he said, suddenly serious. "I think we're gonna earn every dime of it on this one."

"What do you mean?"

Angel said nothing else. He was busy looking out the window. His fifth-floor office offered a bird's eye view of the surrounding blocks. He'd spotted the blue van on the street below, its windshield wipers intermittently swiping at the light rain that now fell from the gray sky.

Chapter Two

Two hours later Angel had to turn up his collar to defend himself from an icy wind blowing in from the sea. The rain, which had fallen steadily, had slowed to little more than an occasional spit from the gray and turbulent sky. He drew a deep breath, raised his eyes, and gazed once again at the building in front of him.

Though he had only worked for the Company for a short time after operations were moved from the Pole, Angel always approached Company headquarters filled with a deep sense of nostalgia—as well as a deep sense of loss.

The headquarters building loomed large on the shore, a full thirty-four stories, its broad base drawing upward in jagged angles toward a point high above Yule Tide. The building was sheathed in green glass and lights twinkled from behind the tinted windows, so that it resembled a gigantic Christmas tree in full ornamentation—opulent and unnatural.

Angel entered the building, passed through the metal detectors, and quietly merged into the crowd of Company employees and tourists who constantly poured in and out of the building that many called "Christmas Central." He bypassed the reception desk and made his way toward the rear service elevator. Next to the elevator, he entered a seldom used stairway and proceeded down to Sub-basement 3 and the production line known as "Electronic Amusements."

As Angel emerged from the stairwell, two large men in blue uniforms were in the hallway, fortunately walking in the opposite direction. He turned smoothly and ducked back into the stairwell. Closing the door behind him, he was just able to read the words "Company Security" on a patch sewn on the sleeve of one of the men.

Angel waited a full minute, then silently opened the door. He made his way down the hallway, hoping all the time that the office of the man he had come to see had not been moved to another floor. After all, it had been some years since he had been welcome at headquarters.

Rounding a corner, he smiled in relief when he found the door with a nameplate that read, "Richard Praetorius." Peering through the window and assuring himself that the occupant was alone, Angel slipped inside.

A long workbench stood in the center of a spacious, well-lit room. On the bench lay a seven-foot-long tube that resembled a sleek metal casket. A tiny, silver-haired man, nearly as small as an elf and wearing a white lab coat, bent over the work bench. The man pressed a latch and the top of the tube rose on hinges to reveal an interior roomy enough for a person to lie within. The small man pressed the latch again, the top lowered back into place, and bright light leaked from around the closure. This light was accompanied by a sound like the buzzing of distant bees. The small man nodded repeatedly, beaming in evident delight. This was short-lived however, for after only a few seconds something thunked loudly, the light was extinguished, and the buzzing stopped.

"Damn," the small man muttered.

Angel closed the door behind him with an audible click and the man turned toward the sound. Squinting through a pair of thick eyeglasses, it took a moment before a smile stretched across the little man's face. "Harold Angel!" he exclaimed, shaking himself excitedly. "What on God's green earth are you doing here? I thought you'd lit out years ago."

"How ya doin', Doc? I see they still got you in charge of electronics down here."

Praetorius shook his head. "They only want me to think I'm in charge. We both bloody well know that. Sure, they keep me around in case I get another idea like the compact disc player or the electric shaver with the three floating heads."

"You're forgetting the Clapper," Angel reminded his friend.

Praetorius bowed slightly. "It's kind of you to remember," he said. "But despite my achievements having garnered me the position of department head, I find my role here to be largely titular in nature." Praetorius lowered his voice conspiratorially. "We both know who's really in charge of everything around here."

Angel nodded his agreement. "What are you working on there, Doc?" he asked pointing to the workbench.

Praetorius ran both hands lovingly along the length of the tube. "I must admit that I had great hopes for this one. This is a combination tanning bed and fully automatic depilatory. Designed to be unisex, this baby features sixteen separate settings. Everything from Brazilian wax to billiard balls. Would have been perfect for the high-end market."

"What happened?"

Praetorius gave his head a doleful shake. "There were some...There were some, um...Some unfortunate results among the test subjects."

"How unfortunate?"

"Can't tell you, Harold. Legal says I can't discuss it until the lawsuits are settled."

"You can't win 'em all, Doc," Angel said.

"Guess not. But I keep trying."

Praetorius motioned Angel toward a chair. When Angel was seated, Praetorius smiled. "You didn't come in here after all this time just to catch up with me, did you, Harold?"

Angel shrugged. "What can you tell me about Luther Deo?"

"What makes you think I know anything about Luther Deo?"

"Doc," Angel began, "you and I have known each other a lot of years, and you know that I know that there is damn little that happens at the Company that you don't know about. Now, I know that what you know is sometimes not official, but it's always on the money."

"Yes, yes," Praetorius giggled, "I guess a man of my talents just likes to be reminded of his importance from time to time."

"There's only one Dr. Richard Praetorius," Angel agreed. "Now, what can you tell me about Luther Deo."

Praetorius leaned back in his chair, placing his fingertips together. "Just before Deo disappeared...You know that he disappeared?"

Angel nodded.

"Well just before he disappeared, I couldn't help but notice that there was something very wrong between him and our current Claus."

"What was wrong, Doc?"

"I don't rightly know. You know that I don't have many good things to say about the operation since the original Claus passed away. And you know that I've got almost nothing good to say about things since the Company bought everything out and moved us all to this prefabricated little paradise on the sea. But one thing I'll say for the Company, they have managed to appoint a couple of mighty fine Clauses since Kringle died."

Angel straightened up in his chair and opened his mouth to speak, but Praetorius raised a hand and continued. "I know. I know. I had some words with Claus the Second, and he was in charge when you left the Company, but looking back on it, I figure that was mostly my reacting to the idea that anybody could take Kringle's place. And you know that Claus the Second didn't have anything to do with the factors that led to your leaving. No. Both Claus the Second and the Claus we have now were good elves, elves who have come up through the ranks, elves who have worked on the line, loaded the sleigh, elves who have been with us through thick and thin, and who somehow, despite all that has happened, have managed to keep Christmas in their hearts. That is, I had thought so until recently."

"What have you got, Doc?" Angel pressed. "What was wrong between Deo and the current Claus?"

Praetorius sighed. "Their relationship had become strained. These two individuals, maybe the last two individuals working for the Company who truly know how to keep Christmas well, began to avoid each other. They began to communicate only by memo. If both were to attend a meeting, one would find some excuse to stay away. There was trouble between them."

"What kind of trouble?"

"I'm sorry, Angel," Praetorius said. "I really don't know."

Angel sat in thought for some minutes. Praetorius sat quietly, watching. Angel lowered his eyes and picked absently at the fabric that covered the arm of his chair. Finally, Angel looked up at his friend. Something glimmered in his eyes.

"Now, watch out, Harold," Praetorius warned. "I've seen that look before. That's the same look you had in your eyes the day you left the Company. The day you—"

"Don't worry, Doc," Angel interrupted. "I know what I'm doing."

"You expect me not to worry? Hah! I'm not supposed to worry," the little man said, shaking his head.

Praetorius paused. "Tell me, Harold," he said at last, "does Scratch know that you're here?"

Angel smiled. It was a thin smile lacking in even the pretense of mirth. "I'm not afraid of Scratch."

Praetorius leveled an uneasy gaze at him. "Everyone's afraid of Scratch.".

Angel made no reply.

Chapter Three

Angel sat at his desk once again staring out the rain-specked office window. Above, a couple seagulls circled lazily. One let loose a load of excrement and Angel followed it down, watching as it splattered white on the hood of the blue van that had followed him from Company headquarters and was now parked on the street below.

He leaned back and listened to the familiar squeak of his desk chair. When he'd gone into business some ten years earlier, he'd rented the office already furnished. The wood-framed chair and large metal desk dated from the 1940s. A file cabinet of a similar vintage stood in the corner, serving as a repository for his case files. The list of accomplishments chronicled therein was short and undistinguished. Oh, he'd helped solve the Gruber case, returning Mrs. Gruber's stolen jewels and even getting his name in the newspaper, but he'd been unable to parlay that success into anything resembling a thriving practice. And that had been eight years ago.

Angel didn't like thinking about the past. When he looked back on his long life, from its empyreal beginnings, his short-lived seat on the Archangelic Council, his demotion and subsequent assignment to the Pole, and how his initial optimism about moving Christmas to Yule Tide had led to his precipitous fall from grace, Angel felt as empty as the promise of redemption.

But he now had a paying customer. And the blue van was evidence that someone was taking an interest in his movements. A man was missing. This was no time to wallow in self-pity. There would be time for that later.

Endless, yawning time.

Angel had asked Billy to see what he could dig up on their client, the leggy Mrs. Deo. Billy eagerly accepted the charge. He grabbed his cap and sped out the door like a hopeful suitor late for the school dance. His assistant could have used the office laptop—an internet search would likely have been sufficient to get at least her curriculum vitae—but Billy preferred a more personal approach. Angel didn't argue with the little man who enjoyed a wealth of sources and possessed a nose for sniffing out details both public and carefully hidden. He likely would not be back for hours.

My turn, Angel thought, and he picked up the phone from his desk.

It took him a while to be connected. At first, the operator balked when Angel asked to speak directly to the Claus. Yes, he knew how important the Claus was. No, his call was not expected. No, he did not work for the Company. Yes, he knew that Christmas was coming. But he traded on what little was left of his status, telling the operator who he was, that he was formerly with the Company, that he had been an intimate acquaintance of the late Kris Kringle, and that he'd known the current Claus since his days on the line.

He found himself placed on hold—as he'd expected—then transferred to another operator who placed him on hold, again, but finally the call patched through.

"Harry," the Claus said in his familiar booming voice. "It is wonderful to hear from you. It's been so long that I wondered if maybe. Maybe...Well, I know it's not possible for you to actually...You know...I...I..."

"I'm alive and well," Angel said. "And gainfully employed. I've been asked to look into the disappearance of Luther Deo."

After a pause, the Claus said at last, "I didn't think anyone outside the Company knew about that."

"I learned directly from the wife," Angel explained. "And although I know that she has reported it to the police, I don't know that she's discussed it with anyone else."

"And she's asked you to look into this?" the Claus asked.

"Yes. And since the missing man worked for you directly, I thought that you might be able to help direct me."

"I can't think how," the Claus said. "His sudden disappearance came as a great surprise to me. I don't know that I can—"

"I find," Angel interrupted, "that speaking with those even peripherally involved with a case can be quite illuminating. If we talk, we might discover some detail, something that might not seem at all important, that could give us a lead." Angel paused. "I know, of course, Mr. Claus, that you want to do everything you can to help."

"Of course, Harry. Of course. And please, call me Santa."

Angel chuckled. "I remember when, before your promotion, your name was Elvin."

The Claus chuckled too. "And I remember you as

20

Mr. Angel."

"Much has changed," Angel said. "Much, but not our commitment to Christmas. And to those who make it possible. Will you speak to me? I have time this afternoon."

Angel heard a ruffling of papers on the Claus's end of the call. "Oh, I'm sorry," he said. "Not today. There's just so much—"

"Tomorrow, then?"

More ruffling. "Tomorrow? Tomorrow? Yes. That might be possible. I've got some time in the morning. Let's avoid the office, shall we? How about the mansion instead? Say, ten o'clock?

"That will do fine. Your house at ten o'clock." Angel paused. "Thank you, Santa."

"Thank you, Harry," the Claus said. "Oh, and it goes without saying that we should keep this just between the two of us. No need to discuss the matter with anyone else."

"Just between us, Santa," Angel assured him. "Goodbye."

Angel put the phone back on its cradle and spun around to look out through the window. The rain had stopped, and the sky seemed a bit brighter. A shaft of light from a small opening in the clouds shone on the blue van still parked below.

"Just between us," Angel repeated.

****

Billy returned to the office in the late afternoon, sporting a knowing grin and scroll of parchment gripped tightly in his left hand. Old habits, Angel thought. Billy insisted on writing his reports on parchment, his tiny handwriting forming lists with bullet points not unlike those that Kringle used to post on the wall of the old workshop at the Pole. The lists of naughty and nice.

"What do you have for me?" Angel asked.

Billy's grin widened. "Plenty, Boss," he said as he unfurled his report. "Our client was born Norma Stapleton in Devil's Lake, North Dakota. Gloria I. Deo is her stage name."

"Stage name?"

"Yeah. You know it's not so uncommon around here. Lots of folks move to Yule Tide and change their names to something that sounds Christmassy. You know Jack Blitzen, the owner of Blitzen Motors? You know, the guy with all the commercials on late night TV? He was born Herman Schlumberger. Changed it to Blitzen. Blitzen's a name with panache. You can practically hear the snap of the whip and the jingle of bells when he says, 'Blitzen Motors! Cars so magical you'll think you're riding in Santa's sleigh.'"

Billy let out a laugh that sounded like it hurt him.

When Angel didn't so much as smile, Billy said, "But I digress."

Angel nodded. "You said Gloria Deo was her stage name. Does that mean she's an actress?"

Billy shook his head. "Nah. She's a canary. You know, a singer. She was anyway. Before she married Luther Deo, she had a job at a nightclub called The Night Visitor. It's over on Vixen Street. Near where it intersects with Fruitcake Avenue? Say, how'd you like to get stuck living on a street called Fruitcake Avenue?"

"Wait a moment," Angel said. "What was her stage name before she married Deo?"

"I just told you," Billy insisted. "Gloria I. Deo."

"She took her husband's last name before she

married him?"

"It seems so."

"It seems odd," Angel said, "like she was either prescient or predatory."

"Luther Deo *was* a fine catch," Billy said. "Guy like him must be pulling down something like three-hundred-and-fifty large. Not including bonuses."

"Tell me about her career as a songstress."

"Sure. Sure. She was pretty popular, from what I heard. Strictly local, but definitely a big fish in the Yule Tide pond. I also heard she used to go out with the owner of The Night Visitor, a guy named Noel Baba. That was, of course, before she married Deo."

"Where have I heard the name Noel Baba before?"

Billy consulted his scroll. "He used to run numbers for Smiling Sammy Bingle. Bingle ran things in the north end. North of Icicle Lane? As you know, after Bingle got rained on, most of his crew lit out. It wasn't exactly safe for them to stick around. But this Baba stuck around. Made out pretty good, too. Somehow got himself a stake big enough to buy The Night Visitor."

"Hmm," Angel hummed.

"Hmm, what?"

"Nobody in this town does anything without Scratch's say-so. I always figured Bingle was rubbed out because he ran afoul of Scratch. I wonder if this Baba had anything to do with that. I wonder if The Night Visitor was some kind of reward."

Billy nodded. "Well, it's a popular joint. Tourists, sure, but also the local hoi polloi. Wealthy Company men. Their wives dripping with ice. But the bent nose crowd, too. You know, wise guys."

"Hmm, again," Angel said. "That's good work,

Billy."

Billy beamed with pride.

"Have you ever been to The Night Visitor?" Angel asked.

Billy's smile vanished. "It's not..." he began, "it's not a place where they...you know." He paused and took a deep breath. "Boss, it's the kind of place that don't exactly let folks like me in."

Angel sighed. There were things that he knew his friend didn't like to talk about. Treatment of elves by humans was one of them. It was no longer as overt as it had been in the first years after the Company moved Christmas and re-established the town. There were even some who claimed it was a thing of the past. Some humans. No elf claimed that. You couldn't be an elf in Yule Tide and get through a day without some slight. Some easily deniable indignity.

Angel forced a smile. "So, how long ago did our client marry the now-missing Luther Deo?"

Billy's smile returned. "Nearly three years ago. It was a Christmas wedding. The current Claus, he was new at the job at the time, he officiated." Billy looked down at his scroll. "By all accounts, the bride was lovely in a white chiffon number, a white jacket with green trim, and a train as long as a runway. It took four bridesmaids to haul the thing down the aisle behind her."

"Sounds peachy," Angel said. "Three years is enough time for the bloom to fall from the rose. Any idea if the marriage is a happy one?"

"The folks I talked to say yes. Deo is absolutely devoted to her."

"And Mrs. Deo? Is she equally devoted?"

Billy's mouth tightened slightly. "Again, the people

I talked to say yes, but…"

"What is it, Billy?"

"It's just that this Gloria Deo has been seen alone on several occasions at The Night Visitor. You know, since the marriage. She even sings there sometimes."

"And when she does, is this Noel Baba in attendance?"

Billy nodded vigorously. "Yes. Most definitely."

Angel leaned back in his chair. "Hmm," he said.

Chapter Four

Santa lived some five miles from downtown Yule Tide in a large structure on a hill with an expansive view of the business district in the distance and the docks and the bay beyond. Although nicknamed the Gingerbread Mansion, the three-story residence of the Claus was built of sturdy redwood. It was a yellow and peach-toned Victorian replete with exquisitely wrought details. Facing the street, the roofline was broken by three gables and a high, shingled turret topped with a needle-like spire. Multiple decks and balconies looked out onto the formal front garden, all enhanced by spindles and ornate curlicues of alternating peach and yellow that looked as though they had been piped on with a pastry bag.

According to its website, visitors were normally restricted to the first floor of the mansion. The upper two floors were reserved and housed the Claus's private residence, as well as offices for staff not stationed at Headquarters. The website claimed over 900,000 visitors each year. More than the Hearst Castle.

Angel had been told to park in a small, reserved lot close to the mansion. A guard in a blue uniform was stationed in a booth at the entrance. Angel gave his name and the guard radioed for instructions. Angel waited until the radio squawked a loud reply. He thought it unintelligible, but the guard nodded and said, "Roger." Smiling, he waved Angel into the lot.

It was a rare sunny winter's day. but a cold wind swirled twigs and tufts of shorn grass along the sidewalk and a line of gray storm clouds could be seen massing in the distance. A long line of visitors, corralled by stanchions and zig-zagging ropes, wended their way from the main parking area, past the garden, and finally to the front porch where several smiling young humans dressed as Santa's elves scanned tickets. Angel avoided the line and instead directly approached one of the faux elves.

"I have an appointment to see the Claus," Angel informed him.

The man blinked rapidly several times, but his smile remained fixed. "Your name?"

Angel told him and the man spoke into a radio he had clipped to his jacket. Angel waited. The man's radio sounded harshly, and he nodded, signaling two other men who stood at silent attention nearby. Angel watched carefully as they approached.

When he had visited years before, guards at the mansion had been outfitted in the same standard blue uniforms worn by both guards at Company headquarters and the guard in the booth where he'd just parked. Apparently, there had been a change.

The two guards coming toward him, although humans, were dressed like militarized elves. They were uniformed in emerald-green jackets with white trim, red pants with black stripes tucked into black combat boots, and instead of the pointy hats worn by the ticket takers, these two wore ballistic helmets made of Kevlar the same color green as their jackets. They also both carried very un-Christmassy M4 carbines. Despite the rifles, they were careful to maintain cheerful grins which, contrasting with their cold and expressionless eyes, Angel found uniquely unsettling.

Santa's shock troops.

After checking his ID, the two security officers led Angel up the front steps of the mansion, through a metal detector at the entrance, and into an enormous lobby with high ceilings, more redwood siding and, against the far wall, a river rock fireplace capacious enough to barbecue a moose. A gift shop to the left of the lobby beckoned shoppers, while a bar and restaurant to the right featured hot toddies and caribou burgers served alongside "Mrs. Claus's famous garlic mashed potatoes."

A guided tour gathered outside the entrance of the restaurant was comprised mostly of parents and small children, but included a few older, unaccompanied adults likely hoping to reclaim some of their childhood Christmas spirit.

Angel hoped they wouldn't be too disappointed.

The tour guide informed the group that their first stop would be the Museum of Christmas located in the rear of the mansion before they moved on to the main attraction—Santa's workshop. Several of the children smiled gleefully at the promise.

The guards bypassed the tour and took Angel through an unmarked door and down a narrow hallway that led to an elevator marked "Private" which was secured by even more guards. The elevator was summoned, the door opened, and two of the guards motioned Angel inside before they accompanied him to the third floor.

More security officers greeted Angel there, but when ushered through an archway and into a spacious parlor, his escort remained outside. The room featured a smaller version of the river rock fireplace and a well-polished and well-appointed bar. In front of the fireplace, a group of four overstuffed leather chairs. two human-sized and two elf-sized, with side tables were arranged in a convivial setting.

"What can I get you, Harry?" a voice sounded.

Angel turned to find the Claus entering from an adjacent room.

Like the Clauses before him, Claus the Third was an elf with white hair and a full beard and dressed in the requisite red suit lined with white fur and a wide-buckled black belt.

Thomas Nast has a lot to answer for, Angel thought.

But this suit was superbly tailored revealing a trim and well-muscled physique. Angel wondered what Kringle—who had truly embraced that belly "like a bowl full of jelly" image—would have made of his well-conditioned successor.

"Would you care for a drink?" the Claus repeated. "I can ask one of the elves to make us some cocoa or, if you prefer…" Cocking his head, the Claus pointed to the bar.

Angel surveyed the bottles that lined the shelves. Spotting a bottle of well-aged, single malt, he said, "Perhaps a small scotch."

The Claus smiled. "You've excellent taste," he said. "How do you take it?"

"In a glass," Angel replied.

There was a button near the end of the bar, the Claus pressed it, and another elf entered the room. He was young. Of course, since elves age so slowly, it was difficult to accurately gauge, but certainly only a few hundred years old. He was of average elfin height, around the four-foot mark, and was dressed impeccably in a tailored three-piece suit—tweed, Scott grey with a subtle check, and a matching tie with a full Windsor against a brilliantly white, French-collared shirt. A blue pocket square emerged artfully from the jacket's chest pocket. If he noticed Angel in the room, it was not apparent.

"Mr. Dickens," the Claus said. "A scotch for my friend. Neat."

Dickens nodded without expression.

Because the bar was built to human proportions, Dickens had to make his way up a ramp to a raised platform that ran behind it.

While his drink was being poured, Angel took a moment to stroll around the room. A large oil by Thomas Kincade hung above the roaring fireplace. Another painting—this signed by Terry Redlin, depicting the Gingerbread mansion in an unlikely snowy landscape— took up most of another wall. On top of a sturdy oak bureau, stained dark like the bar, were several framed photographs. The largest was of the late Kris Kringle, mouth wide in joyous laughter, his arm flung across the shoulders of the elf who had now replaced him. Another was of the Claus and his wife—a tall blonde human woman dressed in a tight-fitting sheath dress of bronzed apricot, sleeveless to show off her well-toned arms.

The Claus wasn't the only one in the family that was hitting the gym, Angel thought.

Angel recalled some of the criticism that emerged when this Claus was first chosen for the job. Some commentators sniffed judgmentally about the world's most famous elf being married to a human woman but most of that was quickly brushed aside. At least in the mainstream media. In the social media such criticism continued to bubble and waft like an ever-spreading pool of excrement.

Almost hidden behind a photograph of the Claus posing with a group of smiling grade schoolers was a shot of him holding hands with Gloria Deo. A man of medium height, thin and balding with an unfortunately unruly mustache and voluminous eyebrows stood nearby staring at them. The expression in his eyes was wary and not at all good natured.

Angel picked up the photograph and the Claus appeared at his side, a scotch in hand. Giving Angel his drink, the Claus said, "I see you spotted Luther and Gloria Deo. Too bad finding Luther in real life isn't as easy." He paused. "We are all worried sick about him."

The Claus reached up and took Angel by his sleeve, leading him toward the grouping of armchairs. Dickens followed them at a distance.

Angel glanced significantly at Dickens.

The Claus smiled. "Oh, I assure you, Harry, anything you can say to me you can say in front of my majordomo. His discretion is above reproach."

"Like his haberdasher," Angel said.

The Claus chuckled. "Yes. Our Mr. Dickens *is* quite the clotheshorse.

Dickens's austere mien remained unchanged. Angel smiled, approached him, and extended his hand. "Harold Angel."

Dickens reached up and placed a strong, albeit small, hand in Angel's. "Fenster Dickens," he responded, his face utterly expressionless.

"Come, Harry," the Claus said, "let's get comfortable."

The Claus and Angel took chairs while Dickens stood silently by.

Angel sipped at his scotch, noticing that the Claus had not had Dickens pour anything for him. "You're not drinking?"

The Claus chuckled. "A bit early for me. I'm afraid I don't have your constitution. As I recall that was a subject of some envy among us elves. I don't think any of us ever saw you in the least bit inebriated no matter how much you imbibed."

"That was then," Angel said. "I had more stamina then."

A moment's fretfulness clouded the Claus's expression but quickly passed. "So, how do think I can help you, Harry?"

Angel took another sip of scotch and glanced again at Dickens before placing the glass on the nearby table. "Did you happen to notice anything out of the ordinary about Luther Deo in the days before his disappearance?"

"No," the Claus replied. "Of course, these are hectic days as we approach our main event. You can't believe the number of details that need to be worked out. Among other duties, Luther heads our logistics committee. Perhaps our most important team. We talked, of course, every day, but as I mostly oversee production, our time person-to-person is somewhat limited."

"And when you did talk, did you notice anything different? Anything troubling him?"

The Claus shook his head. "No. Nothing we haven't dealt with before. He was having trouble getting clearance for us to fly over Venezuela, but they're always like that. They'll come through. They always do.
"

"Anything besides work seem to be of concern for him? His health okay? Did he seem happy?"

"He seemed to be in excellent health. And I wouldn't say he was *un*happy. But Luther is not one to wear his emotions, be they exuberant or melancholy, on his sleeve."

Angel nodded, picked up his scotch, and took a slow sip. "So, you'd say he kept things to himself?"

The Claus cocked his head. "Well, I don't know that I'd put it that way exactly. I'd say he preferred to deliberate on things before voicing an opinion. Not one to jump to conclusions. That sort of thing. It made him appear rather…What's the word? Taciturn."

"When was the last time you saw him?"

The Claus leaned forward in his chair. "It was the day he disappeared. Luther had been in meetings all morning and stopped by my office at headquarters around one o'clock. Strictly routine. There had been a rather large increase in wishes for something called *Cyberslayer Unleashed*. I understand it is a video game. And quite violent. We walk a fine line with those. We want to give the kiddos what they want, but we try not to endorse first-person shooter games. I suggested we substitute more agreeable titles like *The Magical Manatee* or *Tuffy Tiger's Terrific Travels*. He agreed to mull the suggestion over. Then he dashed off and I haven't seen him since."

"He stopped by your office?"

"Yes."

"He didn't call or send a representative?"

The Claus's eyes narrowed. "No. Why do you ask?"

"It's nothing," Angel assured him. "I'd heard that Mr. Deo had been a bit reclusive lately. Missing meetings. That sort of thing."

"This close to Christmas?" The Claus shook his head. "Not likely. Who told you such a thing?"

Angel shrugged. "It's not important. So, the last time you saw Deo you didn't note anything that would help explain his disappearance?"

"Nothing at all."

Angel sipped the last of his scotch then sat rolling the empty glass between his palms. For his part, the Claus sat quietly until, it seemed, a thought struck him. "I remember the next day when I heard that Luther had not reported for work. I remember wondering if maybe he had simply slept in. He'd mentioned that he and Gloria had plans for the evening before. He even invited my Dora and me. They had reservations at a local club. A place called The Night Visitor. Unfortunately, I had a prior commitment. One of our oldest serving elves, Teeny Tuppence, was celebrating a birthday. Nine hundred and seventy-six. After the production line shut down that evening, we had a little soiree."

"Teeny must have appreciated that very much."

"I hope so. They give so much, you know. And ask for so little in return."

"I have fond memories of the production line," Angel said. "The one at the Pole, I mean."

The Claus smiled. "Ah, Harry. That was a thing of beauty. In those days we had thousands of elves crafting millions of toys on the line. Here?" The Claus shrugged. "Since the move, with outsourcing and all, we are down to only a couple of hundred elves producing only a few hundred thousand. Still, the line continues. Mostly for tourists, perhaps, but also as an enduring testament to Christmas."

Angel cocked an eyebrow. "And the elves that are no longer working the line? How are they faring?"

The Claus hesitated, then glanced up at Dickens who was still standing statue-like near them. Turning back to Angel, he dabbed at something in his eye. "Most retired. Some came here with the rest of us. Many stayed at the Pole. There are homes you know. Retirement villages run by the Company just for elves. Everyone is well taken care of I assure you."

Angel nodded but said nothing.

"Is that all, Harry?" the Claus asked. "I've really got to get back to business."

"Just a couple more questions, please, Santa. You mentioned that Deo and his wife planned a visit to The Night Visitor on the evening before he disappeared. Have you ever been there yourself?"

The Claus's eyes widened slightly. "No," he said. "I've not had the…the pleasure. It's not…How do I put this? It's not a place where…"

"It's not a place that welcomes elves," Angel finished the thought for him.

"It is not."

"But surely you being Santa and all?"

The Claus snorted quietly. "Oh, yes. They would undoubtedly have let me in. They'd likely have made a great fuss. Taken my picture. Celebrated my visit. But the next evening if some other elf came to the door…"

"It would not be opened."

"I fear not."

"Have you ever met the proprietor? A man named Noel Baba?"

"A curious name," the Claus noted. "No, that I would remember."

Angel set his glass on the table and stood. "Thank you for your time, Santa."

The Claus rose as well and began to lead Angel out toward the elevator. Dickens followed mutely behind them. "I'm afraid I haven't been very much help," the Claus said.

"You never know," Angel replied. "It might seem that way now, but things have a way of changing. As more facts are uncovered, something you said today might provide a new perspective. Change can be useful." Angel paused and took a last look around the room. "Then again, sometimes things change entirely too much."

The Claus stopped and looked up at Angel, his expression both inquisitive and kind-hearted. He reached up and took Angel by the hand. "It's been hard on you, hasn't it, Harry? These past years?"

"Hard on a lot of us."

The Claus nodded.

"There is one thing that I noticed," Angel said.

"Just one?" the Claus said with a smile.

Angel didn't return the smile. "It looks like you've beefed up your security force here. There are many more guards now than I remembered from my last visit."

The gleam in the Claus's eyes dimmed noticeably. "My, that was so long ago," the Claus reminded him. "But, yes, there have been many changes. Unfortunately, the times we now live in require them."

"Their uniforms have changed as well."

"Yes. Our security chief requested something a bit more…A bit more…"

"Whimsical, yet with a martial flair?" Angel suggested.

"Something like that."

"And the M4s?"

The Claus shrugged and raised his hands in a gesture of helplessness. "I grant that takes a bit of getting used to," he said. "But care must be taken to give our gendarmerie the tools that they need. To keep everyone safe, I mean. Still, they strived for what you might call an elf-like appearance."

"Elf-like?" Angel nodded. "Hmm. Funny you should put it that way. I also noted that they are all humans. Not an actual elf among them."

The Claus frowned slightly. "Elves are happiest behind the scenes."

"And the ticket takers," Angel continued. "The restaurant staff. The clerks in the gift shop. All humans."

"Elves are meant for other things," the Claus said. "Making toys, for example. And did you know that our stable of reindeer will only allow themselves to be bridled by elves. Without them, Christmas would be impossible."

"I'm sure you're right, Santa," Angel said. "It's just...It's just so unlike the way it was. In the old days, I mean. It's not at all like it was at the Pole. There we were, I guess you'd say we were contained. Isolated. No visitors. No gift shops. No humans at all to speak of. Nothing of the theme park mentality that now pervades the operation. This whole town. There, we were our own world. It was...I don't know...more magical."

The Claus released Angel's hand. "I don't disagree, he said. "Emerging from the seclusion of the Pole brought a great many changes. Some good. Our distribution system is much improved and where once children had to imagine what it would be like to visit

Santa's workshop, they can now tour it for themselves. But..." The Claus sighed. "Things that loom fantastical, even enchanted in the mind can, when actually experienced, become greatly diminished."

The Claus leaned forward, fixing Angel with a steady though forlorn gaze. "The thing is, Harry, after a prolonged period of exposure, even the magical becomes the everyday. A remarkably long-lived elf gliding through the air on a sleigh drawn by a team of eight reindeer delivering presents to children all over the world?" He chuckled mirthlessly. "Once you've seen it, worked to make it happen, earned your living from it, it all becomes normal." He sighed once more. "Even the idea that an angel, an actual angel, a visitor from the celestial heights, is part of the operation becomes unremarkable. Sodden and terrestrial."

"Oh, I'm solidly terrestrial these days," Angel said.

"And for that, Harry," the Claus said, "I am truly sorry."

Chapter Five

Taking the freeway back to his office, Angel had no
trouble spotting the blue van following behind him.
Perhaps they didn't care that he knew they were there.
He shook off the thought and, instead of continuing to
the office, took the Garland Street exit and looped back
toward the waterfront. A quick right on Mistletoe and
another on Frankincense brought him toward the docks
and the maze of warehouses and shops that edged the
industrial side of the bay.

Long before it became Yule Tide, this had been a
port city, its residents making their meager livelihoods
largely from the sea. The move from the Pole had
brought not only a new name, but renewed purpose for
the waterfront. Roads had been widened and new
facilities built to accommodate the increase in shipping.
Both new and old were, for the most part, single-story
structures, made of concrete with flat roofs, their grounds
cordoned off by chain link fencing topped with strings of
barbed wire. Semi-trucks lined the streets waiting for
trailers to be loaded and hitched behind them. Along the
shore, towering cranes stood on spindly legs, their long
beaks anxious to peck truck-sized shipping containers
from the unloading ships.

Angel checked his rear-view mirror to ensure that
the van was still following him before taking an abrupt
right into an alley behind a forklift repair shop. Angel

exited the alley and took another right and then another into a small lot crowded with more parked semi-trucks. He managed to find a narrow space between two trucks that provided some coverage and left him an oblique view of Frankincense. After a moment, he spotted the van passing by. Smiling, he pulled out onto the street behind it.

After a little more than a block, the blue van pulled over to the curb. Angel pulled over as well, stopping some twenty-five feet behind the van.

For nearly a minute, nothing happened. Angel sat absently tapping a rhythm on the steering wheel. Coltrane, he realized. "My Favorite Things."

At last, both the van's driver and passenger side doors swung open, two men emerged, and began a slow, tandem march toward Angel's car. The first was tall and thin, dressed in a navy-blue business suit, a light blue dress shirt, no tie, his feet shod in tasseled burgundy loafers that gleamed with a high shine. He was dark complected with a goatee and black hair trimmed close to his temples but left long on top.

The man who accompanied him was far shorter, heavy set, and wore a brown corduroy jacket—thickly padded with a turned-up collar—and heavy-duty blue jeans with a loop on one leg like a carpenter might wear. He sported a flattop haircut and a practiced malevolent stare. His pointy ears and pronounced unibrow made him appear particularly troll-like.

Angel was exiting his car when the van's left side sliding door pulled back and another man loomed forth. This man was enormous. He was some seven feet tall and wore gray sweatpants and a blue XXXL T-shirt that stretched tight over his ape-like chest. His heavily muscled arms rippled, and his thighs so filled out the legs of his sweatpants that they looked as if they had been inflated with a bicycle pump. The big man leaned back impassively against the van as the other two approached.

"Angel," the bearded man said in greeting.

"Balthasar," Angel replied.

"Neat maneuver with the car."

Angel chuckled. "I thought it might be fun."

The short man glared. "Fun?" he snapped. "You making fun of us? You trying to make out we're some kind of joke?"

Angel suppressed a smile. "Why would it be necessary for me to do that?"

The short man growled.

Balthasar grinned. "Settle down, Melchior," he said. "I'm sure that Mr. Angel was just in a sporting mood. Weren't you, Angel?"

Angel shook his head. "Not particularly. I just got tired of watching you watch me. I thought this would be a good spot for to talk. Find out what has you three so interested in me."

Balthasar rubbed his beard with the tips of his fingers. "You know us, Angel," he said. "We're working stiffs. This is just another job. Nothing for you to be upset about."

Angel shrugged. "Oh, I'm not upset. Just curious." He paused. "You working for Scratch?"

Balthasar winced noticeably at the name but recovered quickly. "Come now, Angel," he said. "Like you, we tend to be discreet when it comes to those for whom we work. Suffice it to say we are independent operators, not attached to a single employer. We serve a diverse clientele."

"All of whom either work for Scratch," Angel said, "or are allowed to operate for themselves only as long as they stay in his good graces."

Balthasar made a slight bow. "In which case we, too, would be allowed to ply our trade only if we remain in such a state of grace."

Melchior stared up at his companion, his eyes dull with incomprehension.

"Never mind, Melchior," said Balthasar, "I'll explain it to you later."

"Better use drawings or hand puppets," Angel advised. "I don't think your friend there is much of a verbal learner."

Suddenly, a knife appeared in Melchior's hand. "I'll teach you, Spats," he snarled, advancing.

Balthasar put a hand on Melchior's shoulder to halt him. At the same time, the third man pushed away from the van where he'd been leaning, the vehicle joggling violently as he did.

Balthasar raised a hand. "Caspar," he called, "kindly remain with the vehicle. I'll let you know if we need you."

The big man glowered but stayed where he was.

"You take chances, Angel," Balthasar said.

Angel shrugged. "Some," he admitted, "that I have lived to regret."

"Let's not have this be another," Balthasar said. "Being who you are, we know that we cannot kill you. But there are things worse than death."

"I may know that better than anyone," Angel replied.

"Be that as it may," Balthasar continued, "our client wishes to be kept abreast of any developments in the case you are working. He does not, I'm sorry to say, share much of a concern for your personal welfare. You'd do well to stay on our friendly side."

"Why doesn't your client simply ask me? Or better yet, put me on the payroll?"

Balthasar let out a patient sigh. "Because said client could not be sure that you would share the truth with him. Not the whole truth anyway. No. It's far better that we report what we find as you continue your investigation."

"And if I do something that your client disapproves of?"

Balthasar bowed again. "We would be there to make you aware of such disapproval."

"So, we're in partnership until this thing's over?"

"I don't think partnership is the correct word. But we shall endeavor to provide a guiding hand and sheltering presence on your journey."

"And if I'd rather work alone?"

"Oh, my, Mr. Angel. You know that none of us are ever truly alone."

Angel smirked. "You're wrong, Balthasar," he said, "One thing that experience has taught me is that we are, each of us, ultimately on our own."

Chapter Six

"I don't like them guys," Billy told Angel. "I don't like them being involved. You can't trust a thing that smooth talking Balthazar says and them other two..." Billy paused.

"And the other two?" Angel prompted.

Billy shrugged. "Goons," he said. "They're goons. Ain't got a working brain cell between them, so they make up for it with gutter-level meanness."

Angel leaned back in his chair. The small brass carriage clock he kept on his desktop chimed once. "I'll allow that in the past they have shown a marked penchant for violence."

Billy flapped his arms in disgust. "Penchant for violence!" he repeated loudly. "There you go. Five minutes with that Balthazar and he's got you sounding like him. Penchant for violence! They're goons, Harry. Goons!"

"All right, they're goons. Happy now?"

"Ecstatic," Billy said, his sneer slowly replaced by a soft smile. But as he continued to focus on his employer, that smile tightened noticeably. "They working for Scratch, Boss?"

It was Angel's turn to shrug. "I don't know. I think we'll probably find out before this is over."

Billy shuddered. "Anyway, you ain't told me how the meeting with Elvin went."

"You mean Santa?"

Billy wrinkled his nose. "I remember him as Elvin. And I told you, I can't believe they couldn't have come up with a better candidate for Claus than him."

"You sound jealous."

Billy's eyes went wide with innocence. "Who me? Nah. You kidding? I mean, I do remember some years back when Elvin and I was both up for a promotion to line foreman. So, he plays the corporate game better than me. I got pride is what I got."

"You definitely have something," Angel agreed.

Billy ignored him. "That Elvin? Always so smart, so perfect. Always working out. Always in tip-top shape. What's with that anyhow? And his wife. She's the same. All defined muscles, long legs, and those shoulders? Yowsa! I'll bet she could clean and jerk a Buick."

"Careful, Billy."

"I mean, what's it do to Kringle's memory to have his successor and his wife on the cover of *Shape* magazine?"

"I think they are a very attractive couple."

"The real Santa and Mrs. Claus was an attractive couple. They had natural beauty."

"Kringle was morbidly obese and had a perpetually red nose."

"Yeah, but he did it with class. Didn't have to work out every day to impress everyone."

"I don't think the new Santa works out to impress everyone," Angel said. "I think he does it for his health. Could be if Kringle had taken better care of himself, we'd still have him with us."

Billy shook his head sadly. "I miss him, Boss. I really do. I mean, he fired me and all. But I miss him."

"I do too, Billy."

"So, how'd the meeting go?"

"Well, I didn't learn much," Angel admitted. "Other than that the Claus has good taste in scotch. He insists that he noticed nothing unusual at all about Deo in the days leading up to his departure. Says everything was completely normal."

"But it weren't," Billy said. "Doc Praetorius told you there was something funny going on between Elvin and this Deo."

"That he did."

"And you believe him?"

"I do."

"So," Billy concluded, "Elvin lied."

Angel nodded.

"So, what's our next move?"

Angel stood and walked over to the coffee maker that sat atop the office file cabinet. The warmer had long since clicked off, but there was some coffee remaining. Angel poured it into a cup and took a sip. "We need more information."

Billy leaned forward eagerly. "Where do we start?"

"We have several leads," Angel said. "There's some kind of tie-in with The Night Visitor. The Claus said that Luther and Gloria Deo planned a visit there the night before Deo disappeared. I'll look into that. But it would help if you could dig up everything you can on Baba, the late Smiling Sammy Bingle, and The Night Visitor. Find out if there's anything there we can use as leverage. Oh, and I also want you to look into the background of an elf named Fenster Dickens. The Claus referred to him as his 'majordomo.'"

"Major what?"

"Majordomo. You know, his factotum."

Billy crinkled his brow. "His what?"

"You know, his valet."

"Parks his car for him, does he?"

"No," Angel said, shaking his head. "More like his butler."

Billy nodded. "Gotcha, Boss. What d'ya think this Dickens has to do with Deo's disappearance?"

"I don't know. I don't know anything about him. Let's change that, shall we?"

"You got it, Boss. Right away."

Billy plucked his cap from the coat rack by the office door and smashed it on his head. He opened the door to leave but stopped suddenly. Turning back into the office, Billy opened the bottom drawer of the filing cabinet and drew out a fresh parchment and a quill pen. Grinning, he left the office.

Angel returned to his desk chair cradling his cold coffee. Scarcely more than a minute later the phone rang.

"Mr. Angel, I'm so glad I found you in," Gloria Deo said. "Have you learned anything about my husband and his whereabouts?"

"No," Angel said. "Not yet. Or at least very little. But I do have some additional questions I'd like to ask you."

Angel thought he made out a sharp intake of breath. After a brief silence, Mrs. Deo said, "By all means, Mr. Angel. Ask me anything."

"I'm wondering if we could meet in person."

There was a pause. "Certainly. Where would you like to meet? Your office? I could be there in about a half hour."

"No," Angel said. "I need to go out for a while. Let's

meet for dinner. Say, seven o'clock. I've heard good things about The Night Visitor. It's on Vixen Street. Could you meet me there?"

There was another, much longer pause. "Of course, Mr. Angel," Mrs. Deo said at last. "But let's say seven-thirty."

Angel smiled. "I'll make the reservation."

Chapter Seven

Angel arrived at the restaurant at 7:45 p.m. It was located in a remodeled former auto repair shop—two stories tall, with a red brick façade, fronted by two large rollup doors that, in previous times, had allowed cars to pull in to be serviced. In the summer, the doors could be open and additional tables situated on the wide sidewalk in front. As it was December, both doors were closed but the squares in each had been fitted with windows that allowed Angel to see inside. Business was good. The place was crowded with customers.

Over the doors, the words "The Night Visitor" appeared in large letters. Between the words *Night* and *Visitor* was a plaque with the club's logo—a rendering of a shepherd boy, one arm leaning on a crutch, the other cradling a small lamb.

Angel pulled his car up to the front door and flipped his car keys to a waiting valet. Smiling, he entered the restaurant. Other than the rollup doors, nary a vestige of the former auto repair shop remained. The remodel featured high ceilings, lots of exposed brick, and, in the back, twin staircases on both sides of the room that led up to a wide loft overlooking the main dining area. Several more tables, all seemingly occupied, were set up there. The guests, for the most part, favored semi-formal wear—dark suits for the men, dresses and only a few pants suits for the women. A bar ran about half the length on the right side of the main dining room, reflected light glinting on the mirrored wall behind it. On the left, opposite the bar, a stage was set up for a small combo—an upright piano, a standup bass, and a hollow-body electric guitar sitting there silently.

Like all restaurants in Yule Tide, The Night Visitor had a Christmas theme, but one much more subdued than many others. Above, the crown molding was outlined with garlands of holly and clusters of tiny red berries, and there was a small, heavily flocked Christmas tree in a remote corner, but otherwise it exuded a more timeless elegance.

Angel crossed the small lobby to a station where a short, shapely brunette in a flattering black dress waited, a pleasant but diffident expression on her face. "Have you a reservation, sir?" He nodded and glanced around the room. "Yes. It's under Angel. For seven-thirty. I'm a bit late and I'm meeting someone. Perhaps she is already here?"

The brunette's gaze sharpened as she peered with interest at him. "Yes," she said, "Mrs. Deo is already here. I'll have someone show you to her table."

"*Her* table?" Angel asked. "The reservation is under *my* name."

"Mrs. Deo is a regular and a friend of the owner. She prefers a particular table. It's a preference we try to honor."

Gloria Deo's preferred table was a spacious booth along the right wall far enough from the noise and crush of the bar but with a good view of the stage. It was large enough to accommodate four diners. She sat there alone.

She wore a gray evening dress, the bodice adorned with lace and discreetly placed sequins. The skirt was chiffon. She held a small purse in her lap and was tapping her fingers lightly on the menu that lay closed on the table in front of her. As Angel approached, she looked up and smiled. It was the kind of smile that works equally well as both a greeting and a weapon.

"Mr. Angel," she said, glancing at her watch. "I was beginning to wonder."

Angel knew something of time pieces. Her watch was white gold with a white mother-of-pearl dial surrounded by diamonds and the words Tiffany & Co inscribed at the twelve o'clock position. Likely set her back thirty grand, he thought.

"Forgive me for being late," Angel said, taking his seat opposite her.

Mrs. Deo gave a dismissive shake of her head.

"Nice place," Angel said looking about the room. "You come here often."

It was not a question.

"I do," Mrs. Deo said. "With my husband since our marriage. Before that, I confess I worked here."

"Dishwasher?" Angel asked.

Mrs. Deo smiled that smile again. "I was an entertainer. I'm guessing you know that."

"I do," Angel said. "You gave it up after the marriage?"

"For the most part, yes. I can be persuaded to perform from time to time, but Luther prefers that I not be the center of attention."

"Your husband must be used to disappointment. I'm certain that you are the center of attention wherever you go."

Mrs. Deo started to reply, but Angel interrupted. "That's a lovely dress."

"Thank you." She paused. "Perhaps we should order. Drinks to start?"

"We'd be fools not to."

Angel ordered a scotch and Mrs. Deo a cosmopolitan. The red of the cranberry juice nicely complemented her lip gloss. Angel found himself watching carefully as she took the merest of sips. The waiter returned, took their dinner orders, and returned again with another scotch for Angel. When he departed, Mrs. Deo asked, "Have you any news of my husband?"

Angel set his drink down and leaned back into the booth. "As I said when you phoned earlier, I haven't had much success. Yet. I find that success depends largely on asking the right questions." He paused. "Of the right people."

"Am I the right person?"

"Most definitely."

"Then ask away."

Angel leaned forward and raised his glass. "Do you and your husband share a bank account? Credit card in common?"

"We share everything."

Angel nodded and drank some scotch. "Have you noticed any activity in those joint accounts that might give us a clue as to his whereabouts? Any purchases that might indicate where he is?"

"None," Mrs. Deo said. "No withdrawals or credit card purchases. Nothing. Not since his disappearance."

"Anything suspicious prior to his disappearance?"

Mrs. Deo picked up her cocktail and for a moment seemed lost in thought. She sipped at the drink. "Well, there was one thing. It can't mean much. I noticed that there was a deposit to our savings account about a week before Luther went missing. It was for a hundred thousand dollars. I was curious and asked Luther about it. He told me that it was nothing. A Christmas bonus."

"That's a pretty nice bonus."

Mrs. Deo crooked an eyebrow. "He's had larger."

"I see," Angel said.

"No, it wasn't the size of the deposit that caught my attention," Mrs. Deo continued. "It was the timing. It's not yet Christmas and bonuses have in the past been made just after Christmas. After the deliveries are made, the line slows down, and the hubbub quiets providing a post-season respite."

"So, it was unusual?"

"Not desperately so," Mrs. Deo said, "but, yes, unusual."

The waiter arrived with their meals and nodded at Angel's empty glass. Angel nodded back and the waiter brought him another scotch. Mrs. Deo ordered a Malbec. Before they finished dinner, three men in tuxedos entered from the back of the restaurant and took their places on the stage. Their set began with a soft, instrumental rendition of the Mel Tormé classic "A Christmas Song." "Baby, It's Cold Outside" followed, then "Nature Boy." They were all pleasantly unobtrusive.

The waiter came to clear their plates and Mrs. Deo ordered a Campari. Although his glass was again empty, Angel declined another scotch.

There was a rustle of activity across the room and a tall, thin man also wearing a tuxedo swept in. He had a thick head of unruly black hair, a thin mustache, and as he walked, he waved his arms in front of him as though doing water aerobics. Smiling, he paused by several of the tables, shaking hands, slapping the occasional back, and laughing heartily. When his gaze met Angel's, however, the tall man's smile melted away and something sparked in his eyes. He recovered quickly and was beaming as bright as a lighthouse lantern when he reached the stage.

"Welcome. Welcome. My lovely guests," he spoke too loudly into a microphone. "And thank you all for choosing us this evening. I trust you are enjoying yourselves."

Several of the diners clapped. One tipsy man at the bar whooped loudly and slipped from his stool.

"Fine. Fine," the tall man said. "As some of you know, my name is Noel Baba. I'm the proprietor of this establishment and your humble host.

There was more applause and Baba bowed extravagantly.

Angel turned to Mrs. Deo. "Your friend Baba appears to favor the spotlight."

Mrs. Deo shifted her gaze from the stage and settled on Angel. "You could say that."

Angel grinned. "You could also say that he soaks it up like the litter box of a diuretic Maine Coon."

A chortle escaped her so suddenly that she nearly spilled her aperitif. "You could," she said, "but that would be unkind."

Angel nodded.

From the stage, Baba said, "As your host, I'd like to exercise a bit of privilege and ask an indulgence. I've spotted someone here that has entertained us many times. Always peerlessly. Certainly, one of the finest voices ever to grace The Night Visitor's stage, Miss Gloria Deo."

A small spotlight shining on the stage was turned, illuminating the table where Angel and Mrs. Deo were sitting.

"Perhaps we can prevail upon Miss Deo for a song," Baba said.

When the spotlight hit her, something in Gloria Deo seemed to rise like Venus from the sea. She bowed her head slightly, scooted from the booth, but then strode lithely to the stage. Angel thought her self-assuredness both alluring and potentially dangerous.

She whispered something to the piano player. He nodded and began playing the opening notes of "Have Yourself a Merry Little Christmas." The rest of the band fell in behind him.

Mrs. Deo's voice was strong and clear as glass. Yet as the music played, her confidence softened and a vulnerability that Angel had not seen before slipped through. The lyrics promised that next year all our troubles would vanish into the distance, but her eyes. Her eyes now shone with a deep, unfathomable sadness, brimming with heartache and loss. She looked out not at the audience but rather above them as if beseeching unseen spirits to bring her comfort. It was less a performance than a transformation. She came to completely embody the song with its hopeful lyrics and underlying melancholy. Or perhaps the pull of the song over-swept her. In any case, they were one.

As the song neared its climax, her voice rose to a crescendo and Angel felt a tug at his insides. Something he hadn't felt for ages. He reached for his scotch but found the glass empty. When the final notes sounded, Angel was empty too.

The audience rose to its feet in ovation. Mrs. Deo

bowed to them, then to the band before stepping from the stage. As she returned to the table, several over-eager diners, still applauding approached her, threatening to block her way. Yet, she passed through them unmolested, as though she'd somehow become less corporeal. Like a dream. Or a memory. But it was an all-to-real woman who slid back into the booth across from Angel.

It took him a moment before he was able to speak. "That was remarkable."

She bowed her head in acknowledgment before sipping at her drink.

Angel became aware of several diners sneaking glances at them, glances that quickly turned away if he met their eyes. For her part, Mrs. Deo seemed utterly comfortable with both the attention and the silence that had settled around them.

But, at length, she broke that silence. "Is it true that you were once an…" She paused.

"A Shriner?" Angel said. "Yes, but I had to give it up. I looked atrocious in a fez."

Mrs. Deo smiled patiently. "I'd love to know what it was like. You know…before."

"Before what?"

"Before all of this. Before there was a Yule Tide. Before Christmas was moved. Before."

"It was colder," Angel said.

"No, really," she pressed, her eyes now charged with interest. "I have this vision of life at the Pole with Kringle and the original production line with all the elves and the reindeer and the promise of each approaching Christmas as something out of a…out of a fairy tale."

"No fairies," Angel said. "Elves, yes. Fairies, no."

Mrs. Deo leaned forward. "And angels."

Angel nodded. "Yes. Angels, too."

"Tell me about that."

Angel signaled the waiter for another scotch. "What would you like to know?"

Mrs. Deo glanced down at the table. "What was it like? You know, before. When you were an…You know, when you were an…"

"An angel?" Angel asked.

"Yes."

"I felt much taller."

Angel's scotch arrived and he raised the glass in toast. "To being taller," he said, taking a hearty belt.

Mrs. Deo persisted. "I guess I'm wondering if it were like, let's say, like Dudley, the angel in *The Bishop's Wife*. You know? The movie."

"You've seen *The Bishop's Wife*?"

"Yes."

"What about the remake?"

"*The Preacher's Wife*? Sure, once. But I've seen *The Bishop's Wife* every Christmas since I was a little girl."

"Why not the newer version?"

"Because. Cary Grant."

"And David Niven?"

Mrs. Deo chuckled. "No. Cary Grant. And you are not answering my question. Was it like it was with Dudley? Knowing everyone's secrets and using them to help people make better decisions?"

Angel sighed. "Not exactly, but yes, I had access to secrets. Back then, I knew things. Now, I seek things. The difference is…" He paused. "The difference is meaningful."

"That can't be the only difference," Mrs. Deo said. "Were there wings and harps and celestial choirs? Angels, archangels, cherubim, and seraphim? Can you tell me what it was like?"

"Maybe when I get to know you better," Angel replied.

Mrs. Deo opened her mouth to speak but was interrupted when Noel Baba approached their table. Looking down at Angel, he asked, "Is everything to your satisfaction?" His expression betrayed his utter disinterest. It was not Angel's satisfaction that concerned him.

Mrs. Deo smiled brightly. "Everything is wonderful, Noel," she said. "I should be upset with you for calling me on stage without a whisper of warning, but..." Her smile faded. "I suppose I needed the distraction. This is a difficult time for me. Not knowing. Not knowing what is happening with Luther."

Baba reached out and put a hand on her shoulder before settling in the booth next to her. "You know I'm here for you, Gloria," he said. "As always."

"As always," Mrs. Deo murmured.

Baba turned to Angel. "I understand you've been engaged to help locate Luther." There was a flatness to his tone and dullness in his expression that keenly communicated his lack of confidence that Angel would be any help at all.

Angel grinned. "Yes. You're not the only one who is here for the lady."

Baba smiled tightly. "The difference, I would venture, is that you are on the payroll, while I am here as a family friend."

Mrs. Deo took an audible breath and began to speak,

but Angel talked over her.

"And what's more important than friends?" he asked. "At least the ones who stick by when we need them. You'd know something about that, wouldn't you, Mr. Baba?"

"Whatever do you mean?"

Angel shrugged. "I seem to remember a friend of yours getting into trouble a few years ago. The kind of trouble that separates true friends from hangers-on. Most of this man's associates abandoned him in his hour of need. Well, he's no longer with us, but you...You're still here."

Baba glanced casually, if designedly, about the room. "What friend could you possibly be talking about?"

"A guy named Samuel Bingle," Angel told him. "Smiling Sammy to his friends." Angel frowned dramatically. "Sammy ran into some real trouble. It ended badly for him. Afterwards, it seemed like everyone he counted on was suddenly gone. But you stuck around. Stuck around and...prospered."

Baba stared steadily at Angel. "I'm afraid I don't know who you are referring to."

"And *I* was afraid you'd say that."

"Are you insinuating something?"

"Not at all, Mr. Baba. Not at all," Angel said. "I'm sure you are every bit the friend in need that Mrs. Deo is looking for in this challenging time."

Baba's expression hardened. "That is something you might do well to keep in mind, Angel. I can be a very good friend, indeed." He paused. "Or a potent adversary."

"Thank you," Angel said. "I feel suitably warned."

Baba cheeks flushed red, and he leaned across the table. "I wouldn't be so dismissive if I were you. I may not know this Bingle you mentioned, but I do have friends. Powerful friends. And while we are certainly supportive of your efforts to find Miss Deo's husband, we would be less supportive of your investigation straying into areas that are not your concern."

Angel smirked. "Powerful friends? I know something about friends or at least former colleagues in high places. You may not want to pit yours against mine." Angel paused. "But at present," he continued, "what I need most from you is direction."

"Direction? Do you think I have a clue as to where Luther is? Do you think I'm hiding something from you?"

"Heavens no," Angel insisted. "I'm certain you are being as transparent as you can be. Given your...your circumstances. No. The direction I need from you is very different. I'm wondering if you could direct me to the restrooms."

Baba's eyes clouded with confusion. "The restrooms?"

Angel spread out his hands in apology. "Hey, even angels have to go sometimes."

Chapter Eight

As he left the table, Angel glanced back at Baba and Mrs. Deo. Their heads were inches apart, a troubled expression on Mrs. Deo's beautiful face.

A hallway behind the stage ran to the back of the space. Doors led to the kitchen, what Angel assumed was an office, and the restrooms. Framed photographs were hung along the wall. Most were of celebrities, both local and national, many of them entertainers who had performed at The Night Visitor. Nearly all were signed and featured salutations such as "Thanks for the wonderful evening, Noel," or "To Noel, with love." There was a headshot of Gloria Deo. Across the bottom she'd written, "As Always."

Angel remembered that phrase from the table conversation between Baba and Mrs. Deo. He tucked the memory away as though in a file to be reclaimed later.

The last photo was a crowd shot taken at the restaurant. There were probably a dozen people gathered, some sitting, some standing, some kneeling to get everyone in the camera frame. Front and center stood Baba, his smile perfect. Next to him, standing only about waist high, was Elvin in full Santa regalia. He was not smiling. Next to Elvin, mostly hidden, Angel was able to make out Fenster Dickens.

"Hmm," Angel hummed before entering the men's room.

Angel was surprised to find an attendant and even more surprised that the attendant was an elf. He stood next to a cart topped with Kleenex, mints, a lint brush, and a basket of clean white hand towels rolled like pastries. Like the members of the house band and Baba himself, the elf was dressed in a tuxedo, his accessorized with a bright red cummerbund. He had a prominent nose, red hair, and a neatly trimmed mustache. A nametag on his lapel read "Gabriel."

Gabriel nodded respectfully when Angel entered.

Washing his hands before returning to the dining room, Angel met Gabriel's eyes. Although his expression remained neutral, Angel thought he read recognition in them.

As Angel stepped away from the sink, Gabriel approached with a hand towel.

There was a large basket by the door lined with black plastic. His hands dry, Angel tossed the towel in the basket. Thank you," he said. Taking note of the nametag again, he added, "Thank you, Gabriel. "Angel paused and stared for a moment. "Have we met?"

Gabriel nodded. "A long time ago."

Angel cast back into his memory but was unable to find Gabriel there. "Forgive me. I don't remember."

"No reason you should, sir."

Angel reached into his breast pocket to retrieve his wallet. Hesitating, he said, "Remind me your last name, Gabriel."

"Morningstar, sir. Gabriel Morningstar."

Angel shook his head slightly. "Did you work for the Company?"

"Not the Company, sir. No. Before the Company. In the old days. At the Pole."

"I am sorry. I'm afraid that my memory is not what it once was."

A softness appeared in Gabriel's eyes. "Much is not what it once was."

Angel nodded. "Have you been working here long?"

"Yes. Several years."

"I confess that I'm surprised."

"Why is that, sir?"

"It's just that from what I've been told this place is not…not as welcoming of elves as one might like."

Gabriel tensed visibly. "As I said, sir. I've been here for some time."

Angel smiled sympathetically. "How's the pay?"

"The pay, sir? Rest room attendants are not on the payroll, sir. We are rewarded by the tips given us by our generous guests, sir."

Angel sighed. "Please call me Harry."

Gabriel looked horrified. "I'm afraid I could not…could not do that," he stammered.

"Even if it would give me great gratification?"

Gabriel became even more flustered. "I mean no disrespect, sir."

"None taken. I assure you."

Angel opened his wallet and removed several bills, folding them around one of his business cards. "I'm certainly happy to have become reacquainted with you, Gabriel," he said. "If you ever have need of me, please let me know."

"Certainly, sir," Gabriel said, relief flooding across his face.

Angel leaned forward. "I mean that. I really do."

Gabriel stared at Angel as if searching for something. As though finding it, he said, "I will, sir.

Thank you, sir."

The band was on break, but the club was even more crowded when Angel returned to the table to find Baba gone and Gloria Deo tapping her fingers on the tabletop. She looked at her watch as Angel took a seat. "It's getting late," she said. "I'm sure we both have much to do in the morning."

"True," Angel said. "But it's a shame for this night to end. It's rare that I find myself in such company."

"Perhaps, you need to get out more," Mrs. Deo suggested.

"Perhaps you're right."

Mrs. Deo began to rise.

"We best wait for the bill," Angel said. "We wouldn't want it to look like we are running out on the tab."

"Oh, there is no bill. Noel took care of it."

Angel smiled. "Well, he did say that he and I should be buddies."

"I'm not sure that is exactly what he said."

"If I'd have known he was paying," Angel said, "I'd have had another scotch. In any case, I have a favor to ask."

"What would that be?"

"I was wondering if you might invite me into your bedroom."

Mrs. Deo cocked her head. "That would be quite the favor."

"Indeed," Angel agreed. "And not just your bedroom. Your home. And I don't mean tonight. No. Tomorrow. In the illuminating light of day. I'll even bring my associate. I'd like to search your house. Your husband must have left behind some clue that will help us locate him. I'd like to look for it."

"But I've searched everywhere. I've looked and looked. The police and security personnel from the Company have looked as well. I don't see what you can—"

"Fresh eyes," Angel interrupted. "The fresh eyes of a trained investigator. That's why you hired me, isn't it?"

Mrs. Deo was silent for a moment. "Of course," she agreed. "Tomorrow. Shall we say ten o'clock?"

"Let's do," Angel said.

"Until tomorrow, then," Mrs. Deo said, rising. She smiled at him. That enigmatic smile.

Angel stood and extended his hand. Taking her hand in his he said, "What was it that Dudley in *The Bishop's Wife* said? Oh yes. 'Sometimes angels rush in where fools fear to tread.'"

Chapter Nine

"So, how'd the date with our client go?" Billy asked.

He'd just finished brewing the first pot of office coffee and poured two cups, one for him and one for his boss. Spatters of rain tinged against the window driven by winds that the TV meteorologist had said might reach twenty-five knots. Billy had arrived wearing his rain slicker. It was bright yellow and had a matching rain hat like the one the Gordon's fisherman wears. Billy wore his pulled down over his elf cap.

"I am not dating our client," Angel said, sipping at the coffee. It was strong and bitter, a bit like roofing tar dissolved in mineral spirits.

"That's not what I heard," Billy said.

"And what did you hear?"

"I heard you and the lady was seen last night at The Night Visitor. I heard that she sang a number that liked to bring the house down. I heard afterwards the owner joined you in a booth. I heard he was none too happy you was there."

"You hear a lot."

Billy smiled so wide Angel could make out his molars. "So how was the date?" Billy repeated.

"I wouldn't call it a date," Angel said. "It was strictly part of the investigation."

Billy laughed, a high-pitched squeal that could strip varnish. "Just what are you investigating exactly?" he asked, laughing some more.

Angel stared silently at his friend. After some moments Billy composed himself.

"What have you found out about Fenster Dickens?" Angel asked.

Billy's smile returned. "Plenty!"

He trotted across the office to the corner where he'd placed his scroll. Unfurling it, he said, "Fenster Alabaster Dickens. Age two-hundred-seventy-two, pretty young to be in a position of such authority. Prior to becoming Elvin's…What did you call him?"

"Majordomo," Angel reminded.

"Right. Major dumbo. Prior to becoming Elvin's major dumbo, Dickens was part of the operation's legal team. Got his law degree at the tender age of seventy-five, so he's been at it awhile. The elfin law squad handles everything from complaints about working conditions to negotiating international agreements. Back in the day, they even handled relations with the Archangelic Council. You know, before they cut off relations when the Company took over and moved the operation to—"

"I remember," Angel interrupted. "What do we know specifically about Dickens?"

"He's quite the golden boy. Lots of accommodations, promotions, and the like. Became Elvin's major dumbo two years ago. All reports are that he is…" Billy clasped the top of his scroll and ran a finger down it. Reading, he said *"Dickens is knowledgeable, efficient, and trustworthy, if a bit phlegmatic.* I'm guessing that last part means he's got allergy issues. My sinuses get clogged with phleg every spring. It's the tree pollen. Gotta use a neti pot to clear 'em. You ever use a neti pot, Boss? Disgusting. But it feels great after."

"That's phlegm, Billy. Phlegmatic means lacking in effervescence."

Billy shook his head. "Oh, I ain't got that!"

"And no one would ever accuse you of it," Angel assured him. "So far it all seems pretty dull. I thought you had something on him."

"Oh, I do," Billy insisted. "I dug a bit deeper, and a couple of sources say they think Dickens is mixed up with NAER."

Angel's brow crinkled. "Nair?" he asked. "The hair removal cream?"

"Not Nair," Billy corrected. "NAER. N.A.E.R. The National Association for Elfin Rights. Word is that they wanted to call it E.L.F. for Elf Liberation Front, but some English girl named Granger has the rights to that one."

"Why would it be odd for an elfin lawyer to be involved in an elfin rights organization?'

"Oh, it wouldn't be, Boss. But this isn't just some run-of-the-mill civil rights organization. These guys are pretty militant. At least that's the word. They tried to organize a union at the toy line. When the vote didn't go their way, they tried sabotage. Last year some of them NAER elves broke into the workshop and gummed up the machinery. They poured corn syrup from the candy cane line into the motor that powers the conveyer belt. It took a couple of days before it was up and running again."

"Was anyone caught?"

"No."

"Did NAER claim responsibility?"

"No."

"Then how do you know it was them?"

"It just stands to reason, Boss. At least that's what the Company spokesman said. And the papers. They reported it too."

"So, this NAER is a worker's rights group?"

Billy consulted his scroll again. "Not entirely. They've also made some pretty serious allegations against the Company. You know how when they made the move from the Pole, the Company promised any elf working the line that if they didn't want to come along, they could stay at the Pole? Said that they could stay in their homes free of charge or even move into plush new condos that the Company was building? According to NAER, the Company hasn't kept that promise. They say there's been evictions. That the promised luxury condos are more like prisons. That there have been food shortages. All kinds of things."

"Why haven't I heard about this?" Angel asked.

Billy lowered his head. "Well, it was in the news for a while. But that was a while back. You know, when you was...You was—"

"When I was self-medicating rather more than I should have," Angel finished for him. "I remember."

Billy smiled. "Well, in any case, it wasn't in the news very long because it wasn't true. Them NAER elves was making it up."

"How do you know that?"

"It's not like it's easy to get to the Pole, you know," Billy said "You can't just take a plane. But when the NAER folks started making these claims, the Company took a bunch of journalists up there by sleigh. They toured the facilities. They recorded interviews with elves living up there. They shot video. None of NAER's claims was true. The story was dropped. The press didn't want to print stories that was, whatchacallit, spucious."

"Or spurious," Angel added.

"That neither."

"So, these NAER elves are just stirring up trouble for trouble's sake?"

Billy shook his head. "You can never know what is in another's heart."

"Very poetically put," Angel said. "So, if it were true that our Fenster Alabaster Dickens is a member of NAER, given his important position with regard to the most famous elf alive, that would be troublesome."

Billy nodded. "For him as well as the Company. It would mean that either Dickens is betraying his position by joining in making spucious accusations or that there is something bad going on at the Pole and the Company is not owning up to it."

"How widely shared is this rumor that Dickens is a member of NAER?"

"Oh, I got it on the downlow. Guy didn't want to tell me at all. Had to bribe him. Cost me a fifth of Daniels and a freeplay token I had for the Wolf River Casino in Loleta."

"When were you in Loleta?"

"I weren't. That's why I still had the token."

"You've given me a lot to think about, Billy. Thank you."

Billy beamed, but his smile turned coy. "You want to share anything you learned on your date last night?"

"It wasn't a date. But yes. When I questioned him, Baba claimed he never heard of Smiling Sammy Bingle."

"That don't surprise me none."

"Me neither. But he's not the only one who isn't telling the truth. You remember when Santa told me that there was nothing strange going on between him and Luther Deo before Deo disappeared?"

"Yeah. And you said Doc Praetorius told you otherwise.?"

"Yes."

"Elvin lied," Billy said, a note of triumph in his voice.

Angel nodded. "He lied about something else, too. He told me that he didn't know Noel Baba and that he'd never been to The Night Visitor."

"And?" Billy asked.

"And there is a photograph hanging on a wall in the restaurant showing both Santa and Fenster Dickens posing, albeit none too happily, with Baba and a crowd at the restaurant."

"Elvin lied again," Billy said gleefully. "What do you think he's hiding?"

"I don't know. You were going to look into Baba's background. Got anything for me?"

"Of course," Billy said, handing Angel a scroll. "Good stuff too."

Angel smiled and placed the scroll on his desk beside his carriage clock. Noting the time, he said, "I'll have to read it later. Finish your coffee, Billy. It's nearly time for us to leave."

Billy slurped. "Where we heading, Boss?"

"I managed to convince our client to allow us to search her house. We're to meet her there at ten o'clock."

Billy leered. "Her *house*? You sure you want me to come along? You know what they say? Three's a crowd." Billy let out a peal of laughter that nearly bubbled the finish on Angel's desk chair.

"They also say that an employee who can't quit ribbing his employer may find himself standing in the unemployment line," Angel warned.

"Ah, Boss. You know you could never replace me. We're like two peas in a pod."

"Billy," Angel said, "I find that characterization entirely spucious."

Chapter Ten

Luther and Gloria Deo lived at Snow's End, a twenty-seven-story luxury condominium complex located downtown only three blocks from Company headquarters. Luther could walk to work, Angel thought. If executives of his ilk did anything as pedestrian as walking.

Angel closed his umbrella as he entered the lobby. The rain had continued, and Billy's rubber boots squelched loudly as they crossed the tile floor. A desk blocked passage to a bank of shiny brass elevator doors, each embossed with Christmas scenes—trees, flying reindeer, twinkling stars, and in the center, a stylized Santa climbing into a chimney. A concierge sitting at the desk watched Angel and Billy minutely as they approached.

Angel informed him of their appointment, the concierge picked up a phone, murmured into it, and finally nodded. He then pushed a clipboard across the desk and asked both Angel and Billy to sign and provide contact information. He then checked their IDs against the information they'd provided. Handing back the IDs, he said, "The Deos are on the twenty-seventh floor. The penthouse. You can't get there by the main elevator. You gotta take the VIP elevator around the corner." He pointed. Stretching out a hand, he said, "You'll need this fob to get that elevator to take you there. Please return it before you leave."

Angel took the fob from him and nodded appreciatively.

The VIP elevator opened only at a select number of floors and the fob they had been given allowed access only to one. When they reached the twenty-seventh floor, the elevator door opened directly into the Deos' living room. A surveillance camera pointed at the elevator doors kept track of comings and goings. Across the room, floor-to-ceiling windows looked out onto the bay. Large raindrops splatted silently against the thick glass. The room itself was wide with vaulted ceilings and a ceramic tile floor covered almost entirely by a plush white area rug. There was a white leather sofa and matching loveseat, a white Stressless lounge chair with matching ottoman, glass-topped coffee and end tables, and above the fireplace, hung the largest television set that Angel had ever seen. An image too crisp and clear to be real shown there. Ralphie's father was about to uncrate his prize. "Aaah!" he said, "'Fra-GEE-leh!' It must be Italian!"

The image clicked off as Gloria Deo entered the room.

Angel felt his mouth tighten into a grim line. Seeing Mrs. Deo, a hollow seemed to open within him, and he felt an instinctive need to close himself off.

She was followed into the room by a dog the size of a Ford Fiesta.

Angel recognized it as an English mastiff. Its coat was a fawn-colored brindle. Its eyes were dark and deep within folds of flesh. Contrasting with its lighter coat, the dog's face was black from its eyebrows to the jowls that hung beneath its lower jaw. Angel estimated its weight at upwards of two hundred pounds. When it entered, the dog stared at Angel and shook its massive head. Large flaps of skin hanging from its mouth waved like banners and sent forth strings of slobber. The dog turned from Angel to glare at Billy who still stood by the elevator, rainwater pooling around his boots. A low rumble issued from the dog. Not a growl, exactly, but certainly less than welcoming.

Mrs. Deo approached Angel and offered her hand. Angel took it, bowed slightly, and said, "Thank you again for agreeing to see us, Mrs. Deo."

She smiled radiantly, then looked across at Billy who appeared pinned in place by the glowering mastiff. "Please feel free to remove your coat," she said. "Mr.... Mr.... I'm sorry. Remind me of your name."

"It's um...um, Billy, ma'am," he stammered. "Billy Goodman."

"Come and join us, Mr. Goodman. If it would make you more comfortable, you could remove your boots as well."

Angel noted that she never once glanced down at the mess Billy was making on her floor.

Billy slipped out of his raincoat, then leaned against a wall, and pulled off his rainboots to reveal his pointy slippers beneath. Angel wondered how he'd been able to walk with all that fabric crammed in there.

Billy inched into the room, careful to keep a solid distance between himself and the still grumbling canine.

Nodding toward the dog, Mrs. Deo said, "This is Cuddles. He's my husband's dog."

"Cuddles?" Angel asked.

Mrs. Deo rolled her eyes slightly. "It's actually short for Cuddles G. Willikers. Luther has an idiosyncratic sense of humor."

"Does he…Does he…Does he bite, ma'am?" Billy asked. His voice wavered like a drunk making his way home from the bar.

"Tish tosh," Mrs. Deo assured him. "Cuddles wouldn't hurt a fly."

"It's not flies I'm worried about, ma'am," Billy told her.

Turning back to face Angel, Mrs. Deo swept an arm expansively before her. "You wanted to search, Mr. Angel. Please be my guest."

"Thank you, Mrs. Deo. Perhaps we should start with the bedroom."

Mrs. Deo cocked an eyebrow.

Despite the dog, Billy giggled.

"We're looking for what's missing," Angel said. "Uncovering secrets. Bedrooms are full of secrets."

"They are, indeed," Mrs. Deo agreed.

She ushered Angel toward the back of the suite. The dog remained in place. Billy hesitated, standing in the living room staring after them like a penguin chick whose mother has abandoned him on the ice floe.

"Come along, Billy," Angel called after him. "Never mind the dog."

"That's easy for you to say," Billy said. "A dog that big? A guy my size? He gets hungry, I'd last as long as a tray of rumaki at a sumo wrestlers' potluck."

"Just come along," Angel repeated.

The ceramic tile from the living room carried into the bedroom. Another large white area rug took up most of the floor. The bed was king-sized covered by a fluffy, quilted bedspread—white but stippled with pink and yellow flowers. The head of the bed was piled with more ornamental pillows than Angel could count. Above the bed hung an oil painting of two girls at a piano that Angel judged either an authentic Renoir or the work of a skilled imitator. Twin bedstands flanked the bed. Atop the one on the left sat a CPAP machine.

"Your husband has sleep apnea?" Angel asked.

"Mild, but yes."

"Does your husband travel much for work?"

"Oh my, yes."

"Does he bring his machine with him when he travels?"

"Always. Is that significant?"

"Perhaps."

Angel surveyed the room. Pointing, he asked, "Which chest of drawers belongs to your husband?" Mrs. Deo indicated a five-drawer, Sheraton-style, mahogany with a bow front flanked by two spiral carved columns. Searching each of the drawers Angel found them filled to near capacity.

He then moved on to the adjoining walk-in closet. One side was filled with women's clothes and enough pairs of pricey shoes to make Manolo Blahnik blush. The other side was mostly men's business suits, white shirts, ties, and wingtips and loafers in various tones. Beyond the closet was the ensuite bathroom, complete with an enormous, jetted tub, a tiled shower large enough to bathe a crash of rhinoceros, and twin sinks each with its own medicine cabinet.

Angel felt something cold and wet brush his hand. He looked down and found Cuddles nuzzling him. Behind him, Mrs. Deo entered. At last, Billy peeked into the bathroom, his eyes fixed on the dog.

Angel pointed to the medicine cabinets. "Which one

belongs to your husband?"

"The one on the left."

Angel opened the cabinet. The usual assortment of shaving items and prescription bottles were nestled inside. He closed the cabinet and asked, "Are there other bedrooms?"

"Two," Mrs. Deo answered.

"Show me."

Angel searched the guest rooms. Both were large and featured ensuite bathrooms. One was set up with a king-sized bed and everything needed to make a guest comfortable. Particularly if that guest were royalty. The other was set up as a home office.

Against one wall of the office was a tall mahogany cabinet flanked by twin bookshelves. Examining the cabinet, Angel discovered it to be a Murphy bed. Opposite the Murphy bed was an L-shaped mahogany desk with drawers of various sizes topped with a laptop computer and printer. Next to the laptop was a small, framed photograph of Gloria Deo and a larger framed photo of Cuddles.

Angel smiled. "Is this where your husband works," he asked.

"Yes," Mrs. Deo said. "Well, when he works at home anyway. Naturally, he does most of his work at the office. We like to keep our private time to ourselves but..." She let her voice trail off. After a pause she said, "Work does find a way to intrude, doesn't it?"

Angel nodded. "Do you mind if we look at the computer?"

"Why, no. Please go ahead."

Angel turned to Billy. "More your department than mine," he said.

A grin broke wide across Billy's face and with eager little steps he crossed the room. He sat at the desk and ran both hands affectionately across the laptop before opening it. After a moment, the screen lit up.

Billy's pudgy fingers clicked rapidly across the keyboard. "Password protected," he said.

Angel smiled. "Would you happen to know your husband's password, Mrs. Deo?"

She gave him a demure smile. "It's Lambchop87," she said. "Capital L. The other letters in lower case. Lambchop is sort of a nickname he has for me."

Billy clicked away at the keyboard. Then clicked some more. Then some more. "Nothin' doin. He musta changed it."

"Has your husband other nicknames he might have used?" Angel asked.

Mrs. Deo shook her head. "None that he's shared with me anyway."

"Not to worry, Boss," Billy said. "We're just getting started."

Billy reached into a pocket and removed a thumb drive. Inserting it into Luther Deo's laptop, he shut down the computer, then turned it back on. When the screen lit up, Billy pressed a key on the top row, Angel didn't see which one, and a long list of gibberish glowed in green. Billy scrolled down, chose a line, and began typing what looked to Angel like hieroglyphics. Letters and numbers flashed too quickly across the screen for him to read.

"What is he doing?" Mrs. Deo asked.

"I don't know," Angel said. "But I believe we are about to find out."

Billy shut the computer down and restarted it again. Once light returned to the screen, he clicked and typed and, finally, the home screen appeared. "I'm in, Boss. What are we looking for?"

"Wait a moment," Mrs. Deo said. "What did you do?"

"I reset the password," Billy told her. "It's back to Lambchop87. Capital L."

"Good work, Billy," Angel said. "I noticed that there is a camera set up to record people entering or leaving via the elevator. Can you see if Deo has access to those videos on this computer?"

Billy clicked some more. "Got 'em."

"I like to take a look at everything from the day he disappeared as well as the day before and the day after. Maybe the entire week before he disappeared. We'll want to be thorough."

"What do you think they will show you?" Mrs. Deo asked.

"Probably nothing," Angel said. "But that doesn't mean we don't look."

"That could take you hours," Mrs. Deo said.

Angel nodded. "With your permission, Billy can copy them on his drive, and we can take them back to the office. If you're comfortable with that, of course."

"Already done, Boss," Billy chirped. "The videos are stored on a website. I've got the link and the password."

Angel frowned. "Patience, Billy. She hasn't given her permission yet."

Billy looked appropriately chastised.

"Of course," Mrs. Deo said. "Anything you need that will help you find my husband."

"On second thought," Angel said. "It might be better to simply take the whole laptop. It would give Billy a chance to do even more of his magic."

Mrs. Deo gasped. "Oh, I don't know about that. I have no idea what is on that device. Company secrets, perhaps. I wouldn't want to risk—"

"As I said earlier, Mrs. Deo," Angel interrupted, "we are *looking* for secrets. Mainly the secret of where your husband is right now." He paused. "I assure you, should we stumble on anything unrelated, we will show our utmost discretion. You have my word."

Mrs. Deo hesitated, but only for a moment.

"Yes," she said. "You can have the laptop."

Billy grinned, unplugged the computer, and closed it. He tucked it under his arm and made it maybe three steps toward the door when Cuddles, who had been waiting silently in the doorway, objected with a series of barks loud and resonant enough to dislodge the room's crown molding.

Billy froze. "Nice doggie," he said.

Cuddles added snarling to his thunderous barking.

"Now you stop that, you silly dog," Mrs. Deo said. "Leave the nice man alone."

Cuddles didn't look convinced, but he stopped barking and moved away from the doorway.

"*Elf,* ma'am," Billy, who was still shaking a little from his scare by the dog, said with considerable dignity. "Not 'man.' I prefer elf."

Mrs. Deo caught her breath. "I meant no disrespect."

Billy smiled but his eyes pooled. "I appreciate that, ma'am. It's just not something someone like me can take for granted."

Mrs. Deo did not reply, but her eyes were edged with uncertainty.

As Billy moved toward the pile near the front door

81

that was his raingear, Mrs. Deo drifted back toward Angel. She peered at him as if to ask his forgiveness for her slight against Billy. Angel offered a wan smile and shook his head. Mrs. Deo reached out a hand. Angel fought against the impulse to take it, but as he watched it fall to her side, a part of his soul sighed deeply.

Angel and Mrs. Deo shuffled quietly before the elevator doors waiting for Billy to don his raingear—an operation that took far longer than one would think possible. Angel finally broke the silence. "Oh, I've been meaning to ask you, Mrs. Deo. You took the stage name Gloria I. Deo before you married your husband?"

"Why, yes, I did."

"That's quite a coincidence."

Mrs. Deo shook her head. "Our shared last name? I don't think of it as coincidence. I think of it as kismet."

"Kismet," Angel repeated. "Fate. Such a difficult concept to wrap one's head around."

"In what way?"

Angel spread his hands before him. "It's just that in my line of work it can be difficult to tell the things that are caused by outside forces from those that we, knowingly or not, put in motion ourselves."

Mrs. Deo crinkled her brow. "I don't know what you are driving at."

Angel smiled. "Someone far smarter than me once said, 'I can control my destiny, but not my fate. Destiny means there are opportunities to turn right or left, but fate is a one-way street.'"

"I'm not sure what that means."

Angel shrugged. "I'm not either. But I will say that there have been times in my long existence that no matter how confidently I planned a journey, I arrived at a place decidedly different than my intended destination."

Mrs. Deo smiled. "As an angel, you must be aware of the Serenity Prayer. You know the one. 'God, grant me the serenity to accept the things I cannot change, courage to change the things I can, and wisdom to know the difference.'"

Angel nodded. "I might add, God, grant me the good sense to change course when the path I've chosen becomes treacherous."

"Are you on a treacherous path, Mr. Angel?"

Angel looked hard into Mrs. Deo's green eyes. And at her smile.

"Most certainly, Mrs. Deo," he said. "Most certainly."

Chapter Eleven

As they were leaving the condo, Angel promised Mrs. Deo that he and Billy would be in touch. When Angel returned the elevator fob, the man at the front desk frowned at the sight of Billy leaving with the laptop under his arm but made no further protest.

Billy tucked the laptop beneath his raincoat to shield it from the rain as they walked the short distance to the lot where Angel had parked his car. Driving back the office, Billy asked, "What did we find out, Boss?"

"Not much," Angel replied. "There is every indication that Luther Deo had not planned to be away from home. His medicine cabinet, the clothes packed in his dresser, the CPAP machine. All speak of possible foul play." Angel paused. "Of course, a clever person wanting to cover his tracks might leave all of that behind as a decoy."

"Do you think Deo's on the lam?"

Angel shook his head. "No. Just leaving room for possibilities. We'll know more after we watch those videos, and you search his computer."

Back in the office, he and Billy went to work—Angel accessing the videos on the office computer, Billy minutely searching the hard drive of the laptop for any clue to Deo's disappearance. Although there were not many files related to Deo's work for the Company—those Billy surmised would be accessible only at Deo's office—there were thousands of emails, hundreds of digital photographs—many of Mrs. Deo, many more of the dog—and a lengthy browser history to go through. Angel sat vigil across from Billy, fast-forwarding first through every hour the day of Deo's disappearance, then through several days on either side. Both worked intently, both managed to get a few hours of sleep that night and, significantly, neither had anything stronger to drink than coffee. But by the afternoon of the second day, the pair had to admit defeat.

Billy reported finding nothing substantial on the laptop. After viewing all the video, the only thing Angel knew for sure was that on the morning of his disappearance, Luther Deo approached the front door of his condo, a brown leather briefcase in hand. Angel could clearly make out the initials "LD" engraved in gold. He gave his wife a husbandly peck on the cheek and vanished from camera view not to return. Subsequent video was mostly Gloria Deo coming and going from the condo. Angel smiled as he zipped through the video of the morning that she had visited his office. The silky blue dress she had worn that day loomed large in his memory. But his search of the videos yielded nothing that would help them find the missing man.

Angel glanced at the clock on his desk. Three in the afternoon.

He reached for the phone and dialed. Mrs. Deo answered on the third ring. "Mr. Angel," she said breathlessly, "have you found my husband."

"No," Angel admitted. "We've been through the laptop and, unfortunately, did not find anything to help solve the mystery of your husband's disappearance."

"Is there nothing more you can do?"

"There is always more we can do," Angel assured her. "Since our search of his personal laptop did not prove illuminating, I believe our next move would be to search his office."

"At Company headquarters?" Mrs. Deo asked. An edge tinged her voice.

"Yes. Do you think you could gain us entrance?"

"I suppose I could call over there and let them know you are coming."

"Hmm," Angel said. "I think it would be better if you accompanied us. In my experience, strangers are rarely welcome in the offices of the mighty. Are you doing anything at the moment?"

"Why, no I—"

"Then you'll meet us there?"

Mrs. Deo hesitated. "Dear. It's already mid-afternoon. Perhaps it would be better if we waited until—"

"It's almost Christmas," Angel reminded her. "Surely Company staff are working long hours in preparation for…what is it the Claus calls it? The main event?"

"But I don't know if—"

"Are you concerned that you might not be welcome there?"

Angel could feel the smile rise in her voice. "Oh, tish tosh," she said. "Luther made it clear that I am always welcome to visit. And his secretary is a doll."

"It's settled, then. Meet us there in, say, a half hour?"

Angel and Billy were waiting in the lobby when Mrs. Deo arrived. Her dress was a flowery print with a V-neck, long bell sleeves, and a swingy skirt that ended just above her knees.

There were two desks in the lobby barring access to a bank of elevators. Like those at the Deos' condo, the elevator doors at Company headquarters were brassy and embossed with Christmas scenes. Of the desks positioned before them, the largest was manned by two uniformed guards, one scanning the lobby, another staring intently at computer monitors. The other was an information desk staffed by a young guy with a very full head of chestnut brown hair, dimples, and a suit jacket buttoned so tight across the bottom of his rib cage that his lapels billowed like sails in a stiff breeze. As the trio approached his desk, the man smiled benignly. Mrs. Deo responded with a full wattage beam.

"Hello, Dan," she said to the staffer. Angel was uncertain whether she knew the man's name or was reading his name tag. "Gloria Deo. Luther Deo's wife. I'm wondering if we might just pop up to his office."

The man stared, blinked rapidly, then said, "Your husband is not in today, Mrs. Deo. Is there something I can do for you?"

"No thank you. We'd just like to run up there for a moment. That isn't a problem, is it?"

"I, uh…I, uh…"

"I thought not. We'll just show ourselves up." Mrs. Deo gave one last smile and turned toward the elevators, Angel and Billy following meekly in her wake.

Angel looked back in time to see Dan snatch up a telephone, jittery eyes fixed on them as the elevator doors closed.

It was quite a ride. Deo's office was on the thirty-fourth floor, the very pinnacle of the building, and the elevator ride to reach it was both unearthly quiet and blisteringly fast—somewhere in the twenty-miles-per-hour range. As it ascended, Angel felt his heart drop into his intestinal tract while Billy winced, scooted to a corner, and reached out with both hands to brace himself. Mrs. Deo was unaffected, watching serenely as the numbers on the panel showed the floors flickering by.

When it stopped, Mrs. Deo led Angel and Billy down a corridor, glass walls revealing spacious offices on each side. At the end of the corridor, a door with the nameplate read, "Luther Deo, Operations, Special Assistant to the Claus." Mrs. Deo pointed, and Angel noted what he took for genuine pride in her eyes.

She pushed open the door and smiled at the woman seated at the desk in the outer office. She was in her thirties, pretty, with shoulder-length, curly, blonde hair, and eyes just a bit too far apart, giving her a somewhat vacuous appearance. "Effie," Mrs. Deo said. "We'd like to take a quick look in Luther's office, if you don't mind."

Effie's lower lip trembled slightly. "Oh, Mrs. Deo. I'm so glad to see you. How are you holding up? We've all been so worried about Mr. Deo. Have you any news?"

The words tumbled from her like pebbles down an unstable embankment.

"I'm afraid I haven't any news," Mrs. Deo replied. "In fact, that's why I'm here. These two gentlemen are assisting in our search for Luther. We thought it best to have a look in his office. Who can say? There might be a clue inside as to his whereabouts."

Panic crackled in Effie's eyes. "Oh, but Mrs. Deo. I assure you. Both the police and Company Security have thoroughly searched your husband's office. If there were anything there, I'm certain they would have—"

"Are you saying that I'm not welcome to look in my own husband's office," Mrs. Deo interrupted.

"I'm really not authorized to…What I mean to say is…" Effie kept glancing from the inner office door to Mrs. Deo standing before her, then out through the glass wall into the hallway.

Mrs. Deo leaned forward. "Since when do you need authorization to allow me to visit. That's never been a problem in the past."

"But Mrs. Deo," Effie pleaded. "It's different now. Since Mr. Deo went missing, I've been asked to—"

"To interfere with my search for him?" Mrs. Deo finished for her.

"Not at all, Mrs. Deo. You must understand that I…that I…"

Effie fell suddenly silent as the door from the hallway swept open. Angel turned as Balthasar entered the office. Both troll-like Melchior and hulking Caspar loomed out in the hallway, looking as out of place in the posh environs of Company headquarters as a pair of baboons at a debutante ball. When Melchior caught sight of Angel, he sneered, rancor glittering in his eyes. Caspar only had one expression—glowering menace.

Billy inched around the side of Effie's desk, placing a barrier between him and the interlopers. Angel cocked an eyebrow, but Mrs. Deo glared. "Are you from Company Security?" she demanded.

Balthasar tugged gently at the crisp white cuffs that emerged from the sleeves of his tailored suit coat. "Of a sort, Mrs. Deo," he offered. "I have been asked to insert myself into any situation that might create obstacles to the smooth investigation of your husband's disappearance. I'm afraid that would include visits to

Company property by distraught family members."

"Distraught?" Mrs. Deo repeated. "How dare you! I'm simply doing everything I can to locate my husband. One of this company's most important employees. How dare you interfere?"

Balthasar bowed. "I meant no disrespect, Mrs. Deo. I can see how upset you are. Perhaps it would be better if you withdraw until such time as you are of a more rational, rather than emotional state of mind."

"Listen, buster!" Mrs. Deo said, advancing.

In the hallway, Melchior fumbled at the door, but managed to get it open. As both he and the enormous Caspar entered the office, Angel stepped between Mrs. Deo and Balthasar, his eyes locked on Balthasar's. "Perhaps Mr. Balthasar is right," he said. "A strategic withdrawal might be in order."

Mrs. Deo took Angel by the shoulders and wheeled him around to face her. "You know this man?" she snarled. "Where does he get off keeping me out of my own husband's office?"

"I fear," Angel said, "that Mr. Balthasar is authorized by the highest authority. And as he has seen fit to bring his…" Angel pointed toward Melchior and Caspar. "…his associates."

"Goon squad," Billy interjected from behind Effie's desk.

Melchior took a step toward Billy, but Angel sidestepped Mrs. Deo and moved forward as well.

Balthasar cleared his throat dramatically. "Now, now," he said, "there is no need for all of this antagonism. We all want the same thing. The safe return of Mr. Deo to the arms of his loving wife. How we choose to proceed, however, must be dictated by the

Company. They are, after all, the ones most affected by the loss of an important member of the staff at their most crucial time of year. Histrionics and interference by pseudo professionals can only serve to forestall Mr. Deo's successful return."

Mrs. Deo began to protest, but Angel spoke over her. "And where would he be returning from?" he asked. "You sound as if you know."

Balthasar spread his hands, palms up, before him. "I only wish I did. What I can assure Mrs. Deo is that the Company is sparing nothing in its search for her husband. She can return home secure in the thought that everything possible is being done."

Mrs. Deo stared at Balthasar for several seconds in silence. Angel watched her eyes. They betrayed nothing. Then, all at once, she rushed forward, both hands raised, fingers splayed, nails at the ready and heading straight for Balthasar's disbelieving eyes.

Balthasar recoiled. Melchior and Caspar advanced. But before she could reach him, Angel wrapped an arm around Mrs. Deo's waist and pulled her back. She struggled briefly, but soon calmed.

"I think it best," Angel said, "if we go now."

Grim-visaged and trembling slightly, Mrs. Deo nodded.

She was silent as they rode the elevator down to the lobby. Angel, too, was quiet, watching the floor numbers count down on the panel. Billy's breathing was so heavy he might have been working a bellows.

In the lobby, Mrs. Deo paused, smoothed imaginary wrinkles from her dress, then asked Angel, "What do we do now?"

Angel grinned. "They've left us little choice.

There's something in that office they don't want us to see." He paused. "We'll have to break in."

Mrs. Deo nodded.

Billy just shook his head.

Chapter Twelve

A light rain continued to fall well into the night. Like a solvent, it seemed to dissolve the light from the cars that passed in front of Company headquarters, rendering the street darker than expected. But plenty of light from the brightly lit lobby spilled through the glass doors and across the expanse of concrete at the top of the stairs that fronted the building. Angel and Billy—hunkered down behind a parked car across the street—had a clear view of the two guards stationed inside at the security desk. The guards' attention seemed to be largely focused on a small television they'd set up next to the security console on the desk.

"You sure this plan of yours will work, Boss?"

"Take it easy, Billy," Angel said. "You're just a little nervous."

"Breaking and entering does that to me."

"Just remember, all you got to do is to draw the guards' attention away from the security panel. Doc Praetorius said that when the system is armed, opening any exterior door will flash a warning light on their console. We have the key card he gave us, but when I use it, that light will also alert the guards. I need to know that they will not be in a position to see that light."

"And that's where I come in," Billy said, nodding firmly. "I'll do my best, Boss."

"Just do what I told you and you'll be fine."

Angel slipped away into the darkness and made his way made his way a block down the street before crossing and sliding into the alley along the left side of the Company headquarters building. Billy waited. Angel signaled with a penlight and Billy approached the front entrance.

Peering from the side of the building, Angel watched as Billy in his tattered elf uniform stepped into the full glare of the lights that illuminated the entrance. Reaching the locked glass doors, Billy began to pound both fists against them. "Please!" he wailed. "Please! You've got to take me back! Please! I know what Christmas is all about!"

Billy backed off a few feet and dropped to his knees. A front door opened, and a guard emerged. He stepped cautiously outside, his right hand on his holstered gun.

Billy began to bawl incoherently.

"All right. All right," the guard said. "I need you to stop this disturbance at once. You've got no business here at this hour."

"No business!" Billy sobbed. "I'm an elf. Christmas *is* my business. I know I was bad. That's why they let me go. But I can be better. If they'd only give me another chance."

The two-way radio clipped to the guard's chest squawked. *"Whatcha got out there, Mac?"* a voice asked over the radio.

The guard chuckled. "Looks like we got us a disgruntled former employee," he reported. "No worries. I'll handle it."

Billy lay down at the guard's feet, his sobs becoming plaintive whimpers. "Everyone deserves another chance," he muttered. "Don't they?"

The guard shook his head and pulled a truncheon from a loop on his belt.

Straddling Billy's prone figure, the guard tapped his leg menacingly with the truncheon. "Listen, you little runt," he said. "They don't pay me enough to put up with this shit. You're taking me away from the Warriors game for chrissakes. You don't move along on your own, I'm going to have to persuade you. And you won't like that one little bit."

Billy rose to his knees. The guard took a step back to allow him to get up off the pavement. "Now you're being smart. I'd hate to have to—"

Angel didn't hear what the guard would have hated. Before he could say, Billy still on his knees, delivered a powerful punch to the guard's groin.

As the guard sunk to his knees, he dropped his truncheon but had enough presence of mind to grab at his radio. Rolling onto the pavement, he croaked, "Backup! I need backup!"

As the other guard emerged from the lobby, Billy was already tearing away, as fast as his little legs would carry him, vanishing beyond the halo cast by the lights at the entrance.

Now that both guards were outside the lobby, Angel used the key card to open the side entrance. He closed the door behind him, spotted another door across the hallway marked "Stairway," and ducked inside. The stairwell was narrow and dimly lit with the staircase itself casting a comforting shadow. Angel waited there until he was satisfied that he had entered undetected.

He could not risk using the elevator. He'd have to climb the thirty-four stories one stair at a time. Making his arduous way up to Luther Deo's office, at one point he muffled an involuntary chuckle as he remembered the wings he had lost so long ago. The memory was a vivid one. The soft whoosh of rising, the silent glide, the air whistling past his ears as he dove. By contrast, his footfalls on the metal staircase rang leaden with irony.

Breathing heavily, he paused when he reached the thirty-fourth story. After a moment, he slowly pushed open the door and entered the hallway. The lights were far brighter here. Angel squinted, listened to ensure that he was alone, then made his way down the hall to Luther Deo's office.

The keycard that Doc Praetorius had furnished him would open the door. This close to Christmas, Angel was sure that many Company employees would be working late. Even at this hour. He assumed that entering Deo's office would show on the guard's console, but he hoped that it would not be unusual enough to warrant their interest. Nonetheless, he'd be wise to hurry.

The office suite had been dark, but the lights came on automatically as Angel entered. He made his way around the reception desk, noting there a framed photograph of Deo's secretary Effie standing on a beach with a tall man and a young boy. Her family, Angel surmised.

Crossing the anteroom, Angel once again used the key card, this time to open Deo's inner office. Those lights too came on as he entered. He closed the door behind him.

Deo's sanctum was a large room carpeted wall-to-wall with an intricate pattern of browns and golds with rose-colored highlights. The walls were dark mahogany. On the left, bookshelves spanned nearly the entire wall, some with books, but most crammed tight with three-ring binders, their spines labeled and dated. On the right wall hung a large oil painting of Kris Kringle striding determinedly across a snow-laden meadow, his long red cloak flowing, reaching down to nearly the top of his black boots. He wore a stocking cap on his head and had a bag of toys slung on his back.

Deo's desk sat at the far end of the room, his chair with its back to the huge window that looked out onto the city below. Only a few lights remained burning in the surrounding buildings—bright squares like unblinking eyes keeping watch on the sleeping city.

Angel rounded the desk, his hand reaching for the computer's mouse. When he moved it, the screen blazed. As it did, Angel heard a distinct clunking sound coming from the outer office. Frozen, he stared at the inner office door, waiting for it to burst open. He waited. Then he waited some more. But the door remained closed, and he heard no further sound. He turned his attention back to the computer.

Of course, it was password protected and because hacking the password the way Billy had done at the Deo condominium was not in Angel's repertoire, Billy had instructed him to simply remove the hard drive. Angel placed the tower on its side, removed the screws from the cover, opened it, and disconnected the power cable and the Serial ATA adapter from the hard drive before sliding it out. The entire operation took less than a minute.

Pocketing the hard drive, Angel crossed back to the office door. He paused, placed an ear against the door, and listened. Hearing nothing, he made his way quickly out of the office and down the hall. When he reached the stairwell, he realized that he had been holding his breath.

He exhaled deeply and began his descent to the first floor.

In time, he reached the ground level. Once again, he paused before entering the hallway and listened. He was about to open the door when he heard loud voices approaching. "Don't worry," one of the voices said. "It could happen to anybody."

"Sure," came a reply. "Every day one of us guards lets himself get punched in the nuts by some deranged elf. Every damn day."

Angel had to stifle his laughter as the voices moved off away from the stairwell. After a moment, he moved away himself into the hallway, out the door into the alley, and then into the murky city streets beyond.

Billy was waiting for him where they'd parked his car. "Did you get it, Boss?"

Angel smiled, reached into his pocket, and handed Billy their prize.

Back at the office, Angel sat at his desk, reached into the drawer, and produced a bottle of Fingal's Cave. Not the twenty-five-year-old scotch favored by the Claus, but a welcome enough reward for his night's enterprise.

Nodding, Angel showed Billy the bottle. Billy, who had hooked the hard drive up to the office computer in the corner, shook his head. "No thanks, Boss. Not until I get done here."

Angel shrugged, produced a highball glass from the desk, and poured himself about three fingers of the scotch. Then he leaned back in his chair, listened to Billy clicking away in the corner, closed his eyes, and sipped leisurely at his drink.

He was tired. Climbing the stairs had worn him out. As had memory. He cast back to his thoughts in the stairway. The memory of his lost wings. Lost, he reminded himself, because he had foolishly placed his confidence in the wrong things. In the wrong people. He opened his eyes, shook his head, and sipped some more scotch. Cradling his drink on his chest, he closed his eyes again. He was not sure if he'd actually fallen asleep when Billy's voice roused him.

"I'll take that drink now," Billy said. His voice was edged with frustration.

Angel sat up. "What's wrong?"

Billy stood and flapped his arms in exasperation. "It's the hard drive," he said. "It's been wiped."

"Wiped?" Angel repeated.

Billy nodded. "Nothing on it but a single folder containing a single file. The folder was titled 'Scratch'. The file, if you can believe it, is nothing more than a recipe for figgy pudding."

Angel shook his head and then poured Billy a scotch.

Billy gulped at it, then gave Angel an anemic smile. "Looks like we been played, Boss."

Chapter Thirteen

Angel didn't sleep that night. After sharing a few drinks together both Angel and Billy showed unusual restraint given their night's disappointment. Billy went home, and Angel sat down at the office computer resolved to document everything he had learned so far about Luther Deo's disappearance.

It didn't take long.

He knew that the Company, including the Claus, was hiding something from him. He'd caught the Claus in a couple of lies and someone with access to Deo's office had tampered with the man's hard drive. To what purpose, Angel didn't know.

He also realized that he didn't know much about Deo himself. He knew the man's position at the Company, that he had disappeared, and that he had a beautiful wife who, by all appearances, loved him very much. But Angel didn't know whether Deo had been murdered, abducted, or had vanished on his own. Perhaps something in the man's past would yield answers.

Angel began searching the internet for information on Luther Deo. He quickly learned that before joining the Company, Deo had been a director at BKS International, a Singapore-based global petrochemical company. Deo, whose expertise had been in logistics, had been recruited by the Company five years previously, well after the move from the Pole. He'd been promoted to Special Assistant to the Claus after only two years of service, shortly after the untimely death of Claus the Second and Elvin's elevation to the position of Claus.

Angel found a year-old promotional video on the Company's website which featured Deo. In the video, Deo sat a desk, perhaps the same desk that Angel had burgled earlier that night, answering questions from an unseen interviewer. Deo, his balding pate glowing a bit unseemly in the lights, spoke enthusiastically about the Company, the importance of maintaining Christmas traditions, and his "deeply personal relationship" with the current Claus—an elf with a heart Deo deemed "as big as Christmas itself."

Angel wondered if Deo's eyebrows had been bothering him during the filming. Either that or he had a nervous habit. Deo had repeatedly tugged at his right eyebrow with his thumb and forefinger throughout the six-minute video. As they had been in the photograph Angel spied in the Claus' office, in addition to an unkempt mustache that was more appropriate for a marshal in Old West Tombstone than a modern executive, Deo's eyebrows were also so immoderate that it was a wonder he could see past them.

There was nothing remarkable about the video. Softball questions and canned responses. Except when the interviewer asked about the allegations that were then current concerning mistreatment of elves at the Pole. Deo held the Company line. All the former line elves who had elected to stay at the Pole were well cared for. The retirement village built and maintained at great expense by the Company was luxurious. You only had to visit yourself to be convinced of that. Yes, travel to the

Pole was extremely difficult, but the Company was recruiting a delegation from the news media to fly up there by reindeer-drawn sleigh and that visit should settle the matter. Deo asked the unseen interviewer if he would like to be part of the delegation. The interviewer gushed. It would be the experience of a lifetime. Deo concluded that allegations of Company misconduct toward elves—the lynchpin of their entire operation—were simply lies perpetrated by scurrilous agents bent on undermining not only the Company but Christmas itself.

Deo had done well. Despite the distracting eyebrow habit, he was utterly convincing. But Angel noticed something curious. During the exchange about the Company's treatment of elves, Deo never once pulled at his eyebrow. He did so continually before and immediately after. But not when talking about elves.

Something about Deo's eyebrow habit seemed familiar to Angel. It took a while, but he finally remembered that the character Mr. Sawyer—the nervous, ersatz psychologist in the movie *Miracle on 34th Street* whose inexpert diagnoses earned him a crack on the skull from the film's Kris Kringle—shared the same proclivity.

"Hmm," Angel hummed.

After viewing the video, Angel searched for news articles about the media contingent that the Company had sent to the Pole. The visit had been covered heavily by media companies throughout the world. Angel found dozens of videos and photographs showing a lush complex, elf-sized to be sure, but composed of hundreds of small individual homes grouped closely together comprising what appeared to be a gingerbread village with rooflines and window frames iced in white. There were interviews with grateful elves who could not contain themselves when speaking of how indebted they were to the Company for rewarding their long service with such a comfortable, even sumptuous, retirement. One female elf, a single, appreciative teardrop tracing a line down her wizened face, declared that the late Kris Kringle would be proud to know that the operation that he had long nurtured was in the hands of such a magnanimous organization.

Angel checked website after website finding the same story, the same video, the same photographs, and the same grateful teardrop. The news organizations were different but, with only minor changes, the writing and the telling of the story were nearly identical. The names of the reporters filing the story were also different, but it was clear that they all had used the same source. Angel wondered how many of these reporters had actually visited the Pole.

Angel then navigated to the website for the National Association for Elfin Rights. The NAER site told a much different story. Posted testimonies of dozens of elves alleged that the plush retirement village was a Company invention. These elves maintained that those who remained at the Pole lived in deplorable conditions, hovels that were inadequately heated, forced to survive on a meager inventory of canned meat and vegetables so scarce that they had to be strictly rationed. There were reports of malnutrition, fingers and toes that had to be amputated because of frostbite, and, most grimly of all, reports of a large mass grave on the outskirts of what once was Santa's village.

But Angel's internet search also made it abundantly clear why these allegations were not to be found in other media outlets. Article after article declared NAER to be a domestic terrorist operation whose propaganda arm worked tirelessly to create a false narrative in an attempt to prize concessions from the Company for their members, many of whom were disgruntled former employees dismissed for habitual laziness, timecard violations, shoddy workmanship, and even industrial sabotage. Their so-called allegations were nothing more than "fake news." Legitimate news outlets carrying these allegations would be spreading known falsehoods and giving comfort to enemies of Christmas.

"Fake news," Angel muttered.

Angel knew more than most about Company spin. About how easy it was for the Company to create a public narrative that was completely at odds with reality. Buying into their cover story at the time they took over operation of Christmas is what put him at odds with the Archangelic Council, ultimately leading to his fall from grace and exile on earth. Looking back, it seemed impossible that he could have believed that the Company only wanted to save Christmas. That they were only interested in creating joyful memories for millions of children and their families.

He remembered the first meeting. The first time he'd met Scratch. He seemed so genuine, so exhilarated at the prospect of ensuring that the operation would continue, even thrive, after Kringle's death. Even when he'd been warned, even when he'd been officially recalled, Angel had vowed to stay. To stay and support the mission, the very idea of Christmas. Even after he'd begun to doubt, to wonder if Scratch had other motives, other goals, Angel continued to look for the good and to hope for the better. Wasn't that an angel's job? To find the good and nurture it?

Angel stood and went to the office window. The sky was black and thick with clouds, but a thin line of red was beginning to form on the horizon. Angel grabbed the office coffee pot and went into the hallway to visit the bathroom and to fill the pot with water. Minutes later he sat down at his desk and listened to the soft gurgle of the coffee maker.

He was tired and would need the coffee. He needed to be as alert as possible when, in the daylight, he paid a visit to a known terrorist organization.

Chapter Fourteen

The offices of the National Association for Elfin Rights were located in a single-level strip mall on the edge of town that some wag had named Nakatomi Plaza after the fictional LA skyrise featured in a 90's Christmas classic. It was a small space, maybe five hundred square feet, sandwiched between a vape shop and a nail salon. It alone among the storefronts lacked any kind of Christmas decoration. No holly. No tinsel. Nothing.

As Angel climbed out of his car, he saw a woman entering the nail salon but only caught a glimpse of her from behind. She was tall and wore a dark brown tunic over black leggings and knee-high, black boots with block heels. Her dark hair was curly on top of her head, but the back and sides were close shaven. A shawl, draped across her shoulders, bulged oddly. Either she was particularly broad-shouldered, Angel thought, or she had something underneath there. He felt something familiar about her, but she disappeared into the nail salon before he could decide what that was.

As Angel entered the NAER offices, a shop keepers bell fixed to the top of the door frame tinkled merrily. A long counter at the far end of the room was fronted by an open space, harshly lit by florescent tubes and filled with white plastic-topped tables and folding chairs. The walls were lined with racks of brochures. He glanced at the titles—*Elf Life*, *The Integration Problem*, and *The Truth About Human Privilege* among them.

There was an open door behind the counter that led to additional rooms. A round, steel call bell sat on the counter. Angel gave it a tap and a clear ding resonated in the otherwise silent space. Then he heard someone moving around in back.

An elf appeared. He wasn't wearing the tuxedo that Angel had seen him in previously, but he recognized him as Gabriel Morningstar, the men's room attendant at The Night Visitor.

"Mr. Morningstar," Angel greeted him.

Sudden recognition flashed in the elf's eyes. He gasped slightly and it took a moment before he was able to respond. "Good morning, sir," he said at last.

Angel smiled. "Remember, you can call me Harry."

Morningstar shook his head. "I'm surprised to see you here, sir. Were you looking for me? Is there something I can help you with?"

"Almost certainly," Angel said. Pointing to one of the tables, he added, "Shall we make ourselves comfortable?"

Morningstar made his slow way out from behind the counter. He sighed heavily as he took a seat across from Angel.

"I confess that I'm surprised to see you here as well, Gabriel."

"Why is that, sir?"

Angel shrugged. "As we discussed the other night, I know that The Night Visitor is not particularly welcoming to elves. I assumed that since you worked at the club you had developed what might be called a tolerance for the suspicion and mistreatment of elves that so many humans in this town demonstrate. A tolerance that allowed you to work there."

"That," Morningstar said, "I would never do. Never."

Angel nodded. "How long have you worked here?"

"Oh, no one actually works here, sir. We are an all-volunteer organization."

"I see."

Morningstar looked down at the table, cupped his right hand in his left, and began to rub his thumbs together. Glancing back up at Angel, he said, "If I might be so bold as to ask, if you are not here to see me, what brings you to our offices?"

Angel looked deeply into Morningstar's eyes. "I have a confession to make," he said. "I have only recently been made aware of the allegations of Company mistreatment of elves at the Pole. I've been..." He paused. "I've been what you might call somewhat indisposed for the last several months. Years, really. I'm afraid I've tended to isolate myself from current events. I am now on a case in which the question of the Company and what is going on at the Pole may provide much-needed direction. I am here to find out the truth."

Morningstar stared at Angel for some time. "This case you are on?" he asked. "Can you tell me about it?"

"Of course. I'm looking for a man named Luther Deo. He's gone missing. His wife has employed me to find him."

Morningstar nodded. "I know who he is. He works for the Company." He paused. "As did you, yourself, at one time. Yes?"

"Yes. For a brief time," Angel admitted. "I was fired."

"May I ask why you were dismissed?"

"It's certainly not a secret. I tried to hold management to certain standards. When I discovered that those standards were being compromised, I objected. By that time, I had lost my former status. I was…I was grounded, you might say and, stripped of my angelic connections, I was much less useful to the Company."

Morningstar nodded. "Less useful to the Company," he repeated. "Like the elves left behind at the Pole."

"Yes. Exactly so."

Morningstar glanced around the empty room before returning his gaze to Angel. "I know little of Luther Deo," he said. "I know he was hired well after Christmas was relocated from the Pole, but since I left the line only weeks after Kringle passed, I possess no knowledge of the man, where he may be, or the circumstances surrounding his disappearance." He paused again. "If that is what this is."

"What do you mean by that?"

Morningstar swallowed audibly. "I only mean to say that I know nothing about it."

"Hmm," Angel hummed. "And you never worked for the Company?"

Morningstar shrugged. "Well, only for a couple of weeks. After we lost Kringle and the Company came in, I became disillusioned. I resigned and eventually made my way here."

"But you hear things," Angel pressed.

"What makes you say that, sir?"

Angel swept the room with an upraised palm. "All of this," he said. "You volunteer for an organization that has made some pretty serious allegations against the Company. You wouldn't do that unless you were convinced that they were true."

Morningstar sighed. "We all hear things."

"Tell me what you have heard."

A phone in the room behind the counter began to ring. Morningstar stood, bowed slightly to Angel, then hurried to answer it. Angel tried to listen but couldn't make out much of the conversation. The elf spoke mostly in monosyllables before closing with "Yes. The package has arrived. I have it with me now." After a pause, Morningstar concluded with, "Yes. I think that is the best course of action."

Morningstar returned to Angel, resumed his seat, and asked, "Is there anything else, sir?"

"Yes, Gabriel. Many things. Before you were called away, we were talking about the truth."

"The truth, sir?" Gabriel asked, staring at Angel with guileless eyes.

Angel took a moment to respond. "I can see that you are reluctant to trust me. I understand that. But I hope you also understand that we have a common adversary."

"The Company?"

"Yes. The Company. But more than that. The individual in charge of the Company."

"Surely you don't mean the Claus."

Angel chuckled. "You know that I don't. I mean the individual who is truly in charge."

Morningstar lowered his head. "I've never met that individual."

"I have," Angel said. "I considered us to be quite close at one time. I put my faith in him. It turned out that in that I was mistaken."

"I have heard things," Morningstar said. "Terrible things."

"Is there anything in particular that you have heard that you think I should know?"

Morningstar was silent for several moments. "This person you seek," he said at last. "This Deo. He was promoted at a time when the Company found itself in a most challenging position. Just after the death of Claus the Second."

"Yes," Angel said. "A tragedy. I know that the poor elf wasn't in his position very long, but I've heard good things about him."

Morningstar brightened. "Oh yes, sir. Claus the Second was a good elf. A good Claus. He wanted only the best for his workers. And for those in retirement at the Pole." His expression clouded. "This, I think, put him at odds with some within the Company."

"Odds?"

Morningstar shook his head. "I only meant to say that his loss was a tragedy. Nothing more."

Angel nodded. "A reindeer accident. Wasn't that the story? Claus the Second died in a freak reindeer accident."

Morningstar huffed quietly but, Angel thought, disparagingly. "That's what they said. Yes, sir."

Angel leaned forward. "And what do you say?"

Morningstar stood and took a few aimless steps along his side of the table. "I believe I have already said more than I should have." Pointing to the racks of brochures lining the walls he continued. "Since beginning my volunteer service here. I have come to understand more than I once did about the nature of truth. Truth is, dare I say it, 'fungible.' Different versions are traded like tchotchkes as if none have any meaning except to distract." He paused. "I believe in the truth this organization is telling. That which this organization stands for. Fights for. But exposing this truth has not resulted in greater acceptance of elves in this town or in this country. Nor in a better life for elves. And certainly, it has not brought help to those abandoned at the Pole. No. Rather we are labeled miscreants. Terrorists. Liars. This has made me...skeptical of others."

"What are you saying, Gabriel?"

"I'm saying, sir, that I am no longer as trusting as I once was."

Angel eyed Morningstar narrowly. "And this lack of trust? That would include me?"

Morningstar nodded. "You may be just as you say you are. But you may be otherwise."

Angel smiled. "I find your prudence commendable, Gabriel."

"Thank you, sir."

"Perhaps after you have known me longer you will be convinced that I am on your side."

"Perhaps, sir."

Angel rose and held out his hand. Morningstar stared at it briefly before taking it in a handshake. "You know what they say?" Angel said. "The truth will out."

Squeezing Angel's hand more firmly, Morningstar replied, "And I find your optimism commendable, sir. Unfortunately, I've also found that people believe most ardently in what they wish were the truth. Whereas the actual truth, like the cry of a trapped miner, is but a muffled echo sounding from a cavern of the damned."

Chapter Fifteen

Angel exited the storefront, stepped into the parking lot and was reaching to open his car door when the blue van squealed to an abrupt halt behind him. As the van's door slid open, the gargantuan figure of Caspar emerged. Both the driver and passenger side doors also opened; Balthasar and Melchior slipped from their seats.

"Caspar," Balthasar said, "kindly help Mr. Angel into the van."

As the big man closed in, Angel ducked low to avoid the larger man's grasp. As he did, he delivered a blow to Caspar's solar plexus. He gave it everything he had but instead of doubling over, the giant simply grinned. As Angel backed away, Melchior rushed toward him, the blade of his knife winking. For his part, Balthasar was content to remain by the van, his eyes gleaming with malice. Angel tried to dart back toward the building, but before he could take more than a step, Caspar swallowed him up in a bone crunching clench. Struggling, Angel found himself being inexorably dragged toward the open van door.

A covering was pulled down over his head. Now blind, his arms were wrenched behind him, his hands bound, and he was tossed in the back of the van. He heard the harsh shriek of the van's door sliding shut and the vehicle lurched forward. Angel tried to raise himself into a sitting position but was pushed down onto the ridged metal floor as the van spun out onto the road.

It wasn't a long trip. Angel estimated only about six minutes. The van slowed to a stop and Angel once again heard the metallic screech of the van door. Hands on both sides pulled him outside and onto his feet.

Melchior laughed as he yanked the covering from Angel's head. The covering was overkill. Angel could clearly see where they had taken him. They were standing in a narrow alley. Angel faced a trash container bulging with refuse, flies swarming above. He turned to find a red brick building and a door, gray metal and pocked with rust spots, that led inside. A small sign over the door read "The Night Visitor."

Melchior, mouth open, lips parted in a vile rictus, said, "Man wants to see you."

Balthasar, a gun in hand, nodded and pointed toward the door. Caspar shoved Angel forward.

There was a rush of air and a flicker of movement behind him, and Angel's hands were suddenly free. He raised them, staring with disbelief as though they were not his own. Eyes darting and heads wheeling like unbalanced turbines, Angel's captors tried vainly to determine what had freed him. But nothing stirred in the alley except the flies over the dumpster. Melchior produced his gravity knife, the blade emerging with a practiced flip of his wrist. He stepped away from the van into the middle of the empty alley, peering down its length. He was about to turn back around when, with a whoosh, a figure appeared only an arm's length in front of him.

It was the same woman whom Angel had spied earlier entering the salon next door to the NAER offices. She smiled at Melchior, a kind, unwary smile. Then she dipped abruptly, pivoted to her left, and brought her right leg up to deliver a devastating roundhouse kick to Melchior's temple. He crumbled to the ground, his knife clattering on the sidewalk near him.

Caspar, seeing his friend go down, lurched toward the woman, hissing as he approached. The woman waited, expressionless, her dark eyes placid pools. Compared to the hulking Caspar, she looked tiny, even frail. But then she stepped forward, extended a single hand, and shoved Caspar back so violently that he crashed into the brick of the building with a crack like a small earthquake. As Caspar sunk to his knees, minute bits from the wall drifted down around him like pixie dust.

Balthasar stepped forward still holding his gun.

The woman turned to Angel, cocked her head, and smiled. Angel returned the smile, nodded, and rushed toward Balthasar. Swinging to his left, Angel hooked Balthasar's right arm and let his momentum swing him around behind his opponent. Holding tightly to the arm, Angel wrenched it upward. The woman winced at the sickening snap it made. Angel let go of Balthasar's arm and took the gun from his useless hand.

Approaching the woman Angel said, "I thought that might be you." He paused. "You changed your hair."

The woman bowed slightly and ran her fingertips through the closely shaven right side of her head. "Do you like it?"

"I do," Angel said. "And I truly appreciate your watching my back."

"Always," she replied.

Angel smiled again. "Would you like to get coffee, Michael?"

The woman surveyed the scene. Melchior was unconscious on the pavement. Caspar sat with his back to the wall of the club, a string of drool hanging from his slack lips. Balthasar was still on his feet but moaning as he clutched his right shoulder.

"Sure," Michael replied. "Nothing left to do here."

"Unfortunately, my car is still parked back where these boys picked me up."

"We could walk," Michael suggested.

"I have a better idea."

Angel returned to Balthasar. "Your keys, please," he said.

"I don't know who this lady is," Balthasar sputtered, "but you two just bought yourself more trouble than you can imagine."

Michael stepped forward and grinned at Balthasar "Trust me," she told him, "I've been dealing with assholes like you literally since the beginning of time. And you have no idea what I can imagine."

The steeliness of her tone froze Balthasar. He stared blank-faced for a moment before handing Angel the van keys.

He was still staring at them as they drove off in his van.

They soon arrived at a coffee shop only a few blocks from Angel's office where he was an infrequent customer. Called The Warm and Fuzzy, it was dark with booths upholstered in deep brown leather, the air redolent with the homey aroma of yeast and cinnamon.

Inside, Angel led them to an empty booth near a window that looked out into the parking lot. Before taking his seat, he said, "I'd offer to take your wrap, but—"

"But people might stare," she said.

"Wings do draw attention."

"They do."

"What can I get you?" Angel asked as Michael took a seat.

Across the room, a barista stood behind a counter trimmed with shiny garlands atop a well-stocked case filled with assorted pastries both sweet and savory. Angel ordered a soy latte for Michael and opted for a flat white for himself. As the barista fixed their drinks, Angel glanced up at a large television set playing above the counter. On the screen, eight-year-old Kevin McCallister was "eating junk and watching rubbish." When the barista set his drinks before him, Angel pulled out his wallet and placed several bills on the counter. Nodding toward the TV screen, he said, "Keep the change, ya filthy animal."

The barista smiled crookedly and gave a knowing shake of his head.

Angel returned to the booth and set the drinks on the table. Taking his seat across from Michael, he said, "I really do like the new do."

Michael tossed her head. "It's sweet of you to say so," she said. 'I confess I cut it short more for practical rather than aesthetic reasons. It's better for battle. As you know, I wore it long for millennia, but more recently I've decided to ignore the more gender specific and go with the strictly utilitarian."

"You've always been beautiful," Angel said. "And formidable."

"And you've always been an impossible flirt."

"Can I help it if I'm inextricably drawn to feminine beauty?"

Diamonds of mirth danced in her dark eyes, then suddenly glinted like razors. "And yet," Michael said, her voice taking on a disagreeable edge, "I've been depicted as a male for centuries."

Angel shrugged. "Human artists have shallow paradigms. Neither they nor their patrons could imagine a female, and a beautiful one at that, yielding your kind of power. Michael the defender. Michael the advocate. Mightiest of the four. If they'd portrayed you as your true self, then—"

Michael laughed. "Their testes would have shriveled at the very thought."

"They would at that." Angel took a sip of his coffee, then leaned forward. "As hard as it is for me to admit my current limitations," he said, "I must thank you for intervening on my behalf back there. I was overmatched."

"My pleasure, I assure you."

Angel cocked his head. "But I must ask, why were you there? To what do I owe such concern?"

Michael stirred at her coffee with a thin plastic swizzle. "You've always been a favorite of mine, Harry." She paused. "You know I argued on your behalf before the council."

Angel smiled. "And I appreciate that, Michael. I really do. But I've come to realize that the council made the right decision. My disobedience could not be overlooked."

"But where there is repentance, we must forgive."

Angel chuckled. "I really thought I was doing the right thing, you know?"

Michael lifted her cup. "I know."

Angel sighed. "After Kringle died, it seemed the

light had gone out of Christmas. When the Company swept in with their promises, it seemed that the light was about to return. I believed them. I truly believed them. I believed Scratch."

"We warned you," Michael reminded him.

Angel shook his head. "I know. Believe me, I know. And you were right. But I wouldn't listen. Even when things began to turn, even when I realized just how deep the betrayal had been, I held on to hope. Hope that I could somehow stem the tide."

"You were proud, Harry," Michael said. "It is something that comes with the territory. Angels are proud. And justifiably so. But too much pride brings blindness. The council saw your pride as hubris. Hubris that had to be punished."

"When I realized that Scratch had brought only darkness," Angel said, "I thought I could shine a light. Hold the darkness at bay. I thought I could be the balance. The bringer of light." He chuckled. "I never had a chance."

"Well, Harry," Michael said, "I believe you still have some light in you."

Angel smiled crookedly. "Only dying embers."

"With proper kindling, that is enough to light up the sky."

Angel stared deeply at Michael and felt a stir of hope. Hope long abandoned. "Is it enough to claim redemption?" he asked.

Michael took a sip of her coffee. "This case you are on? How do you feel about it? How do you feel about getting involved with the Company again? With those who brought about your fall?"

"I brought that on myself, Michael."

She shrugged. "It's not an easy thing, doing battle against the dark."

"You would know," Angel said.

"And yet battle we must, lest the light be overcome."

"Yes. But if my fall has taught me nothing else it is that the devil works in both the light and the dark."

"True," Michael agreed. "But let's forget, for a moment, about light and dark. Let's instead talk about a way forward. You've sidelined yourself for so long. Now you've accepted this case." Michael took another sip of her drink. "Everything happens for a reason," she continued. "At least that's what the optimists say. I say that you are on a path. Luther Deo is on that path. But so is Scratch. It may be the right path for you. It may not. Other paths are available. My advice? Find that one that leads home."

"Home for Luther Deo?"

"Perhaps."

Angel paused. "Home for me?" he asked.

"I wish I could tell you, Harry. All I know is that it will lead you where it does. And that will have to be enough."

Chapter Sixteen

"So, you're telling me that Balthasar and his goons tried to nab you and you was rescued by the freaking Archangel Michael" Billy shrieked. "The *real* Archangel Michael?"

"That's what I'm saying," Angel told him.

Billy was so pent up he had to do a little pirouette in the middle of the office floor to settle himself. "The Archangel Michael?" he repeated, incredulous. "The commander of the army of God? The angel who, sword in hand, cast Satan out of heaven?"

Angel nodded. "Yes. But she left the sword at home. Would have been a bit showy under the circumstances."

Billy's eyes bulged slightly. "The Archangel Michael is a chick?"

"Female angel," Angel corrected him.

"What else ain't you tellin' me?"

Angel smirked. "You have no idea."

"Wait a minute! Wait a minute!" Billy said. "Why did those guys try to grab you in the first place? It ain't like we're making any progress finding Deo."

"I'm afraid I don't know."

"I don't like it, Boss. I don't like it one little bit."

"I confess that I found it a little disconcerting myself."

Billy twirled again. "Well, did you get anything for your trouble? I mean, are we any closer to finding this

Deo fellow?'

Angel leaned back in his office chair. "I'm afraid I don't know that either. But today's events do give us a couple of things to ponder."

"Well, go ahead, Boss, ponder away."

"Let's take things in turn." Angel pulled a yellow legal pad from one of the desk drawers and began making a numbered list. "There have been allegations of mistreatment of elves at the Pole, spread primarily by an organization called the National Association for Elfin Rights. Allegations which, of course, the Company denies. I then visit the NAER office and find it staffed by an elf I met recently at The Night Visitor."

Billy leaned in. "Anyone I know?"

"His name is Gabriel Morningstar. Ring any bells with you? He told me that he is a former line elf who left the Pole shortly after Kringle's death. Your tenures there would have overlapped."

Billy doffed his cap and ran a hand through what little hair he had left. "Let me think," he said, digging his fingernails into his scalp. "Gabriel Morningstar? Well, Morningstar is a common enough elfin surname. And Gabriel? Well, the name Gabriel is pretty common too. You know, like the angel Gabriel, the messenger of God?"

Angel smiled patiently. "I do know. He's an old acquaintance."

Billy winced, took his cap in both hands, and wrung it like a washrag. "Oops. Sorry, Boss. I forgot for a second."

"No problem. But do you remember *this* Gabriel Morningstar?"

Billy shook his head. "I'm afraid not. There was so

many of us at the Pole. It's like asking somebody who used to live in Chicago if they knew so-and-so from Logan Boulevard. Chances are pretty slim."

"Understood." Angel made a notation on the legal pad. "This Morningstar impressed me as a pretty thoughtful elf. Especially for someone volunteering for a so-called 'terrorist' organization."

"But did he tell you anything that will help us with your girlfriend's case?" Billy smiled wide enough to reveal bits of the fried egg sandwich he'd had for lunch still clinging to his bicuspids.

"I do wish you'd stop referring to our client as my girlfriend," Angel said. "We are, after all, looking for her missing husband."

Billy lowered his head. "I was just trying to keep things light."

Angel stared at him a moment before offering a smile. "I forgive you. And, yes, although he was certainly less than forthcoming, I believe he did let slip a couple of things that might be useful in our search."

"Like what, for instance?"

Angel made another note on his legal pad. "What do you remember about the death of Claus the Second?"

Billy's eyes narrowed. "Just what everybody else knows. After, what, about seven years in the position, he died in a tragic reindeer accident. At least that's what the papers said. Why? Did Morningstar tell you something different?"

Angel shook his head. "Not in so many words. But he did bring it up. Right after telling me that he knew nothing about Luther Deo or his work at the Company, Morningstar made a point of reminding me that Deo was promoted to Special Assistant at the time of Claus the

Second's death."

"So what?" Billy asked. "The Claus dies, a new Claus is appointed, and that new one selects a new special assistant. Seems natural to me. I mean, if I was elected Claus, I'd like to choose my own team." He paused. "Whaddya say, Boss? Fancy being my assistant when I get the job?"

"In that unlikely event," Angel said, "I'd be most happy to take the position. Someone would definitely need to keep an eye on you." He smiled at this friend. "But seriously, it strikes me as significant that Morningstar brought it up. Almost as if he were trying to lead me somewhere."

"Where?"

A corner of Angel's mouth curled pensively. "I don't know. But somewhere." He made another note. "And then there was the phone call."

"The phone call?"

Angel nodded. "While we were talking, the phone in the back room rang. Morningstar got up to answer it. I didn't make out everything, but I heard him tell the caller that the package had arrived. That it was there in the office."

"So? What's unusual about getting a package?"

"Only moments later, Balthasar and his boys showed up. Could be it was Balthasar that Morningstar was talking to."

"You think? Some kind of signal?"

Angel shook his head. "Not really. Just trying it on to see if it fits."

Billy shrugged, not just with his shoulders, but with his entire upper body. "But none of this fits. Why would a volunteer from NAER help a thug pick you up and take you to a restaurant where he works as a men's room attendant? Because this Noel Baba told him to? And what did Baba want with you anyway?"

"Who said it was Baba that had me snatched?"

Billy flapped his arms in frustration. "Stands to reason, Boss. Baba's the owner. Morningstar owes his livelihood to him. Baba says 'jump,' Morningstar says, 'how high?'"

"Could be," Angel agreed. "But everything appears to lead back to the Company. Baba, like everyone else in this town, owes his livelihood to them."

Billy shook his head. "Not everybody, Boss," he insisted. "Not you."

Angel smiled. "Okay, not my livelihood. But there is a debt. A debt I'd like to see paid off."

"Whatcha getting at, Boss?"

Angel made a final note on the legal pad. He did it with a distinct flourish.

"I'm saying it's time to quit dancing around this and head directly to the source."

"The source?"

Angel fixed Billy with a stare. "I mean, it's time for me to talk to Scratch."

Chapter Seventeen

A central hallway ran the length of the thirty-fourth floor of Company headquarters extending from Luther Deo's brightly lit office at one end to a distinctly different office at the other. While Deo's suite looked out into the hallway through a set of wide windows, the opposite office was totally closed off. There, the wall was a featureless, dark gray plaster with a massive, windowless door set in the middle. Like the gleaming brass doors of the elevator that Angel used to access the floor, this door too was covered with images. But while the elevator doors were embossed with cheery Christmas scenes, the door to this cloistered space featured a rendition of Flemish painter Jan van Eck's famous diptych depicting the crucifixion and the last judgement. Particularly disturbing was van Eck's rendition of Hades with a sword-wielding Archangel Michael standing atop a hellscape where a skeletal figure keeps occupants in place—occupants who writhe in agony as they are devoured alive by various demons. Not exactly sugar plums and candy canes.

Nevertheless, as he approached the door, Angel had to smile. Van Eck had, of course, painted Michael as a male.

Angel wondered at the ease with which he was able to get this appointment. He'd simply called, was transferred to Scratch's secretary, and was told to come by as soon as was convenient. Mr. Scratch "would be most happy to talk with you."

The door to Scratch's office had no window and no doorknob. There didn't appear to a camera peering out into the hall, but Angel would have laid odds that there was one hidden somewhere. Particularly as when he reached out to knock, the door swung open on its own.

It was dark inside. Not pitch black, but dim. Diffuse lighting, gray as the dusk of a cloudy evening, leaked in from the edges of the room, rendering the furniture inside indistinct, bulky shadows. To the right, a fireplace as cold as a catacomb took up much of the wall. To the left was a bookcase, its murky shelves lined with relics that Angel could only just make out. Set in front of windows blacked out by heavy curtains, the outline of a large desk appeared at the far end of the room. Angel listened but the room was utterly silent. He glanced back toward the outer hallway and when he did, the door began to close. The wedge of light that streamed into the darkened office narrowed then disappeared altogether like the view from the inside of a casket as its lid is fitted into place. As the room slunk into darkness, a small, swing arm desk lamp switched on and in a meager halo of light, Angel made out a figure sitting behind the desk.

"Welcome, Harold," Scratch said. "It has been a long time."

Scratch's voice was just as Angel had remembered it—guttural and singed with melancholy. When they had first met, and Scratch was recruiting him for the Company, Angel mistook this melancholy as a need for connection. He had long ago recognized that, instead of loneliness and a desire for companionship, it signaled the absence of even the possibility of joy. Incongruous for the head of an organization ostensibly dedicated to the exuberance and promise of Christmas. But then, Scratch was no ordinary executive.

"It has been a long time," Angel agreed. "As though from another lifetime."

"I feel that too," Scratch said. "But then, it is not unusual for past lives to intrude on the present. In any case, it is good to see you, dear boy. To what do I owe the pleasure of this visit?"

"I think you know, Mr. Scratch. I've come to ask about the disappearance of Luther Deo."

Scratch sighed audibly. "I am disappointed. I had hoped that you had come to ask for your old job back."

Angel shook his head. "You know that I would never do that."

"Never," Scratch said, "is a very long time."

In the light of Scratch's desk lamp, Angel recognized the large tome, ancient and bound in hand-tooled black leather, that had also occupied the top of his desk in the Company's first days at the Pole. As it had back then, that volume, the desk lamp, and a quill and ink pot were all Scratch kept there. Angel had never seen what was inside the intricately designed covers. He wondered if anyone beside Scratch had.

Scratch turned the beam of the desk lamp to illuminate a guest chair set before him. "Please, dear boy, have a seat."

Angel shook his head again and managed a chuckle. "You know I've always wondered why you call me that. *Dear boy*. It's so charmingly patronizing. Particularly since you and I are of a similar age."

Scratch scoffed. "We were once of a similar rank as well. You serving your master and me serving mine. But while I have prospered in my service, you, if I may say so, have become greatly diminished. Pity. I had hoped for a different outcome."

"I didn't come here for your pity," Angel said. "I came for answers."

Angel approached the desk. As he did, he felt a chill. He shivered as it passed through him. Scratch's face was still in shadow, the beam from the desk lamp shining instead on the book cover. In the slanting light, the raised edges of its filigreed design glowed. Angel felt strangely compelled to touch it.

"The answers you seek," Scratch said, "you'd have them if you returned to work for us."

Angel reached out to the desk and turned the beam of the desk lamp enough to make out the outline of Scratch's face. The high cheekbones, thin lips, and piercing dark eyes were very much as Angel remembered them. New was his thinning hair and even more sallow complexion. He looked almost frail. Angel knew better than to take this as weakness.

"Do you really expect me to believe that you'd want me back?" Angel asked. "Before I lost my status, you exploited what I now recognize as my naiveté to influence the council. Now that I'm grounded, I can't believe that I could be of any use to you at all."

One corner of Scratch's mouth curled. "You lack vision, Harold. Yes, it was unfortunate that the council clipped your wings. But I understand their lack of trust. In those early days we were just finding our footing. Mistakes were made and trust was lost. In the Company, in me, and, ultimately, in you. I also understand that this trust must be earned back. With you in our employ, I'm certain that, in time, we could do just that.

"Not likely," Angel said.

"Don't be so sure, dear boy. It's clear that your former colleagues maintain a great interest in you. You need only to consider the events of this morning."

"This morning?"

"Of course. You found yourself in a difficult situation and the divine intervened."

"You know about that?"

"Naturally. You cannot expect something as pivotal as the captain of the heavenly hosts visiting my city to escape my attention."

"No," Angel agreed. "I suppose not."

"And isn't that visit," Scratch continued, "proof enough that time heals divisions? That redemption is possible? That one day our disagreements will be put aside, and we will once again work together for the betterment of all?"

Angel smiled. "You can't believe that your co-opting of Christmas will ever be forgiven."

Scratch chuckled. "Of course, I can. Your problem, Harold, is one of perspective. You are not seeing the whole picture. You must look at these things as one does a chess game. You concentrate on a single move at your peril. When you see the whole board, not just the next move but the one after that and after that, you realize that loss is acceptable as long as you remain in the game. You lost your wings, but the real loss came when you walked away. A reversal of fortune is always possible right up until checkmate is declared."

Angel closed his eyes. He'd become aware of a humming sound, barely audible, which seemed to emanate both from very far away and quite nearby. Feeling slightly faint, he wondered if he was falling ill.

Despite his abnormally hardy constitution, that had happened occasionally since his fall from grace. But thus far only when he was, as they say, in his cups.

Angel opened his eyes and took several steadying breaths. "Forgive me, Mr. Scratch, if I disagree with you. The way you and the Company twisted Kringle's operation from one that brings joy to children the world over into one that brings you and yours profits and power will never be embraced by the Archangelic Council. You've earned their lasting enmity, and should they decide that a change is in order, they have the power to make that change. Remember, even your master was no match for them. He is where he is because he was driven there. The real power is not with him, or with you, but with them."

"Again, dear boy, your vision fails you. You see my master as having been driven from heaven. I see him as having inherited a kingdom of his own. Much like the way that the Company inherited the operation of Christmas. And both are as strong as they ever were. Stronger. Children still rise on Christmas morning to gifts under the tree. Happy parents revel in their smiles. And this town that we have created, unlike the former operation at the Pole, is accessible. Something that can be touched. A living, breathing place that can be experienced bringing joy to those who visit." He paused, inching the beam of the lamp so that it shone more fully on the black leather cover of the book on his desk. "In addition, as you note, profits are up."

"How nice for you."

Scratch waved a hand as though brushing away an insect. "I understand your skepticism, Harold. But what you fail to understand is how seriously we take our responsibility for the proper execution of Christmas. It is a trust that the Company has vowed to safeguard against anything or anyone that would present a stumbling block. Christmas, as you understand better than most, is a sacred thing. And our vow to keep it secure is also sacred."

"Sacred?" Angel scoffed. "How can you even use the word? I'd think it would turn to ash in your mouth."

Scratch chortled. "Hardly. Despite our commercial success, everyone here at the Company understands that Christmas remains sacred. A celebration of…of…" He paused. "How do you beings put it? A celebration of Immanuel. God with us." Scratch swallowed, then wrinkled his nose as though he'd tasted something unpalatable.

Angel chuckled. "You'd do better to keep God out of this. God might take offense and you wouldn't like that. And as fascinating as I find your worldview, Mr. Scratch, as I mentioned, I am not here to be convinced that your machinations have resulted in a new and improved version of Christmas. I'm here to find out what you know of the disappearance of Luther Deo."

Scratch extended a hand and drummed slender fingers on the surface of his desk. "I wish I could help you. I really do. The Company has spent time and, I'll admit, quite a lot of money attempting to locate this most important member of our staff. But, alas, all for naught. Frankly, we've come to suspect foul play. How else can we explain his sudden disappearance particularly at this time of year? Christmastime. When he is needed most."

"You're saying his absence is deeply felt?"

"Certainly. He is, after all, the special assistant to the Claus."

Angel smirked. "How ever are you coping?"

"I will excuse your sarcasm, Harold. For the moment at least. Let's just say that although dear Luther's absence has caused ripples in the smooth operation of Christmas, even if he does not return in time, no child will be disappointed come Christmas morning. Christmas, like always, will endure."

"Like it did after Kringle passed," Angel said. "Or Claus the Second."

"Yes," Scratch agreed. "Both were singular tragedies with consequences dire. Yet the Company proved itself nimble enough to compensate for even their loss. Of course, we will continue to pursue every avenue in our search for Mr. Deo. We owe it to him. We owe it to Christmas."

"As will I," Angel vowed.

"So glad to hear it, dear boy." Scratch paused. "Is there anything else?"

Scratch grinned, more wince than smile, and the chill that Angel felt earlier returned, but much more intensely. Like an icy cloak, it enveloped him, then plunged deep. He shivered, numbing fingers clutching at his insides. His vision clouded and he feared he was about to lose his balance. He placed a hand on the desk to steady himself and the merest edge of a finger brushed against the leather of the volume that lay there. Angel suddenly felt as though he were swirling, the room itself dissolving, as some powerful force pulled at him, tugging him into darkness.

Angel closed his eyes and pushed back from the desk, struggling to remain on his feet. It was as if the air had been sucked from his lungs. He took several deep, ragged breaths and waited for strength to creep back into his quivering limbs.

"Are you all right, dear boy?" Scratch's voice sounded as though from a distance.

Angel opened his eyes to find Scratch still seated at the desk mere feet from him. It was several seconds before he was able to speak.

"Yes," Angel said, his voice little more than a quaver. "I'm all right. And yes. Questions. I have, uh…questions."

"That's delightful," Scratch said. "But are you sure that you won't take a seat? You seem a bit…a bit woozy."

"I appreciate…" Angel huffed. "I appreciate your…your concern. But I'll be fine."

He wobbled but remained standing. Wiping a palm across his face, he found beads of sweat clinging to his forehead. His cheeks felt enflamed. He continued his slow, deep breathing.

"Your questions, then," Scratch prompted.

Angel kept him waiting until he found sufficient strength to continue. "I'm wondering," he began, "if you could tell me why critical documents from Luther Deo's computer have gone missing? Documents accessible only by people working for you?"

Scratch snorted. "That's right. Security informed me that Mr. Deo's hard drive had gone missing. We suspect that someone from outside the Company was involved. Perhaps a burglar. Possibly you could explain this outrageous intrusion on Company privacy. We're quite at a loss."

"The problem isn't that the hard drive went missing," Angel said "but rather that it had been wiped clean while still in the Company's possession.

Eliminating any clues that it might have contained. Clues that could potentially lead to the missing man."

"And you would know this how?"

"Quit playing, Mr. Scratch. We both know the answer to that."

Scratch nodded. "Yes. Yes, we do. I think we also both know that too much knowledge is a dangerous thing."

"Dangerous? Yes, potentially. Secrets come to light have been known to topple empires. Speaking of, what do you know about allegations of mistreatment of elves at the Pole?"

Scratch spread his hands wide. "Dear, dear. Once again you disappoint me. It appears that you have drunk deep of the pool of conspiracy theory." He shook his head. "Really, I don't know where you are getting your information, but the Company has nothing to hide. Our service, not only to this community but to the world, is well documented and by the most trustworthy sources. This nonsense about mistreatment of elves has been repudiated by every legitimate news-gathering organization in the world. By repeating these fanciful allegations, you are not merely leaving yourself open to charges of slander, you are making yourself the fool. Donning a dunce cap and declaring to the world, 'Hey, look at me.' Not the act of the Harold Angel who was once trusted by the highest authority to safeguard Christmas. But then, as we have already noted, you are not the Angel you once were."

"I'm forced to agree," Angel said. "I'm not who I once was. But I am learning not just to live with my weaknesses, but to find new strength within them."

Scratch leaned back in his chair and smiled. "What

a delightful fantasy," he said. "I'm truly excited to see how that works out for you."

Angel took his time in reply. "I'll be sure to keep you informed. As surely as I will get to the truth. No matter what plans it might scuttle. No matter what empires it might topple."

"My, my, dear boy, that sounds rather like a threat."

"Not a threat, Mr. Scratch," Angel assured him. "It's a vow."

Chapter Eighteen

Angel stood at the bar, one foot on the rail, and sipped at his scotch. It was after four o'clock—happy hour—and The Night Visitor was filling up with a well-heeled crowd drawn by the promise of discounted libations with names like the Candy Cane, Mistletoe Martini, and a neon green concoction called the Grinch. Across the room, the stage was empty, but music played as unseen speakers piped the Louis Armstrong and Benny Carter classic "Christmas in New Orleans" throughout the room.

The bartender had poured Angel's scotch, then made his way to the end of the bar, picked up a silent telephone, and spoke briefly to someone. Minutes later, Noel Baba emerged from the hallway that led back to his office.

A tentative smile played at the edges of Baba's mouth as he approached. "I'm surprised to see to you in here, Angel," he said. "Will our Mrs. Deo be joining you?"

Angel set down his glass. "No," he said. "I'm here solo." He paused. "I was under the impression that you wanted to chat with me."

Baba's smile bloomed and he raised an eyebrow. "Really? How ever did you come to that conclusion?"

Angel lifted his glass. "Let's just say that earlier today three friends of yours somewhat forcefully conveyed the message that you'd like to see me."

"Three friends? I don't know what you mean."

"Of course not," Angel said draining his glass.

The bartender appeared and cast a nervous glance at the boss before addressing Angel. "Can I refresh that for you, sir?"

Angel nodded. "And please get something for Mr. Baba. On my tab, of course."

Baba shook his head. "I appreciate the offer, Angel, but I'd rather not be beholden to you."

"In that case make it two on your tab. I'd never turn down anyone who offers to stand me a drink."

Baba cocked his head and peered at Angel. Turning to the bartender he said, "Two scotches, Jack."

The bartender poured the drinks and placed them in front of the men before withdrawing. Angel raised his glass as though in a toast. "See," he told Baba. "We can be friends."

Baba raised his glass in return. "I'm not sure this makes us friends."

"Drinking companions then," Angel replied. "And I'd venture that a taste for good scotch isn't the only thing we have in common."

"Really?"

Angel nodded. "We've both made a commitment to Mrs. Deo. Me to find her husband and you to…How exactly would you characterize your relationship with her?"

"We are old friends."

"And her husband?"

"What about her husband?"

"Are you two also old friends?"

Baba sighed. "I don't know what you are getting at,

Angel. Gloria used to work for me. She's quite a talent and I was disappointed to lose her. But she met Deo and, as they say, love won out. But despite the end of our professional relationship, Gloria remains a dear friend. And someone of whom I am very protective."

Angel held up his glass to the light. The amber liquid glowed warmly. Like the sky after the sun slips below the horizon. "That's something else we have in common, Baba," he said. "There are others."

Baba set his glass down on the bar, his eyes scanning Angel disparagingly. "Other things in common? I can't imagine."

Angel sipped his scotch. "We also share a somewhat tenuous relationship with the Company."

Baba smiled. "There you are wrong, Angel. I have no relationship whatsoever with the Company. Aside from serving their employees when they visit us here."

"Hmm," Angel hummed. "I did some checking. When this property was a service station it was owned by Samuel Bingle. On paper anyway. Smiling Sammy ran it less as a service station and more like a clubhouse. Grease monkeys worked on cars here in the front. Back there…" Angel gestured toward the back of the building. "Back there he could usually be found in conference with his, I guess you'd call them his colleagues. Dealing cards and tending to his business interests. Word is that some of Sammy's interests conflicted with those of the Company. Sammy was asked to bring those interests into line. He declined. A few days later they pulled his car out of the bay. Sammy was in it. He hadn't drowned. He'd been shot. Multiple times. Word is that someone dropped a dime on him. Someone he trusted lured him out to the docks where…" Angel paused. "Well, the rest is history."

"What does that have to do with me or with the Company?" Baba asked.

Angel shrugged. "After Sammy's unfortunate demise, the bank took possession of the building. The First National Bank of Yule Tide. Interestingly enough, a Mr. Nicolas Scratch sits on the bank's board of directors. Shortly after Bingle's death, the bank proffered a loan, at a very favorable interest rate, to...Well, to you, Baba."

Angel finished his scotch and set it down on the bar next to Baba's.

Baba's mouth congealed into a grim line, and he breathed heavily through his nose, his nostrils flaring like the neck flaps of a lovelorn lizard. "As you say," he said at last, "it's history. Ancient history. The Night Visitor is a legitimate business and I'm a legitimate businessman. I'm not responsible for what happened to the former owner of this property."

"Of course not," Angel said. "I never meant to imply otherwise."

"Then why bring it up?"

Angel spread his hands in a gesture of helplessness. "Earlier you said that you'd rather not be beholden to me. I understand that. A legitimate businessman such as yourself, especially an ambitious one, would chafe under such an obligation. Especially if that obligation were rather more significant than, say, who gets the next round. For example, if I owed my livelihood to another and that someone took advantage of this obligation by asking me to act in ways that are potentially detrimental to that very livelihood, I would be hoping for a change."

"I don't know what you are talking about, Angel."

"Don't you? You see, I don't actually think that you wanted Balthasar and his thugs to bring me here this morning. I can't see how that would be to your advantage. I think that you were acting under orders and simply had no choice in the matter. And I think that if you were given an opportunity to change the dynamic, to wipe clean the slate and remove any obligations that you are now forced to work under, I think you'd welcome that opportunity."

"You're babbling, Angel."

Angel chuckled.

The club's sound systems began to play Etta James' "This Time of Year," her strong and smoky contralto wafting along with Cedar Walton's piano and Red Holloway's dream-like saxophone as though flowing in a slow stream. Angel closed his eyes, listened momentarily, then turned to Baba. "You should know that I had a most illuminating meeting with Mr. Scratch this afternoon," he told him.

Baba stared, then picked up his scotch, and drank deeply. "What business is that of mine?"

"Perhaps none at all. But then again, you might be interested to know that Scratch offered me my old job back."

"Why would he do that?"

"He sees it as an opportunity. He had little use for me before this morning, but since my former colleague came to my aid, he now sees renewed potential in a partnership. I have you to thank for that, Baba. She would not have come to my rescue if you hadn't had them pick me up. Again, I'm assuming that you were working under orders, but when you sent those enforcers to fetch me, you inadvertently changed the dynamic. And

I believe that, under this new dynamic, you and I might be able to work together for our mutual benefit."

"What benefit is that?"

"I'd like to see the Company under new management. I think that if we were able to wrest control from Scratch, not only would there be relief from old obligations, but new opportunities would emerge for us."

"Going up against Scratch would be folly," Baba said.

"I don't think so. I think he's left himself vulnerable."

Baba leaned forward. "Vulnerable? How?"

Angel signaled the bartender for another scotch, waiting in silence until it was placed before him. He sipped, then turned back to Baba. "This thing at the Pole," he said. "If true, it would be most damaging. The Company relies if not on the goodwill of the population, then at least on their ignorance. If we could show that Company executives, specifically Scratch, have not only lied but have mistreated elves in the pursuit of profits thereby denigrating Christmas, the outcry would be seismic. Enough to force a change in management. Enough to force Scratch into retirement. After all, the Company needs Christmas. It doesn't really need Scratch. Rulers topple. Empires endure."

"Scratch has successfully controlled the narrative thus far," Baba observed. "People believe what they want to believe. And although everybody loves Christmas, not everybody loves elves."

Angel narrowed his gaze.

Baba shrugged. "It's just a fact," he said. "I don't make up the facts. You can't seriously be asking me to risk all that I have built on account of some unemployed elves."

"I'm asking you to consider what greater gains might result from a partnership. And I agree with you. You don't make up the facts. Neither do I. Right now, the Company does. I'm wondering if that can be changed. Particularly if we can find a way to remove Mr. Scratch from his current position."

Baba picked up what remained of his drink, stared at it, then finished it off with in a final swig. "Scratch in retirement?" he asked. "I can't see him leaving the Company for a quiet life in the country."

Angel gave him a crooked smile. "It's possible that the end of his tenure at the Company would come more quickly and more finally than that. Public disgrace is likely not something his employer would tolerate."

"And if Scratch is gone, what then?" Baba asked. "He might be replaced by someone worse. It wouldn't profit me to start over with someone new and potentially even less friendly to local business interests."

"But with me back in my position with the Company, in the event of Scratch's departure, I would be able to provide a moderating influence."

"Seems like an iffy proposition."

Angel nodded. "It does. And I'm not asking for you to sign off on it. Or even to help it come about. I'm only letting you know that if sudden change occurs, your interests might be best served by that change."

"But why dial me in at all, Angel? If you are not asking me for anything, why tell me any of this?"

Angel sipped some more scotch. "Because, as you say, you are protective of my client. I've come to believe that the best way to serve my client, to uncover what has happened to her husband, is to go after Scratch. To expose his secrets and, ultimately, force him from power. It is a plan not without danger. Danger for me and danger for Mrs. Deo. Should I fail, I'd like to believe that someone would remain to look after her. Should I be successful, I believe that we would all greatly benefit."

"You're a fool," Baba said. "Scratch demands absolute fealty. Even the hint of disloyalty would be ruinous. For you, for Gloria, and for me."

"Ruinous? Like what happened to Claus the Second? Or Luther Deo?"

Baba's eyes flashed with alarm. "I don't know what you are talking about," he insisted. "I just try to keep my nose clean. Something you should think about, Angel."

"I'm not asking you to do anything to betray Scratch's trust," Angel said. "Just to realize where your interests may lie should a change be in the offing. And to protect your 'dear friend' should I be unsuccessful."

"That you can count on, Angel."

Angel smirked. "I know. As always."

Baba stared at him for a moment, then turned and walked away.

As Angel picked up his glass, the restaurant's sound system began playing Tony Bennett's rendition of "Silver Bells"—the one where he is backed by the Count Basie Big Band. Angel nodded along, marveling as he always did at Monty Alexander's piano solo. Then he drained his glass and headed out to the street.

He wondered if Baba would go straight to Scratch. Or would he wait to see what develops? In any case, Angel had planted a seed. It was a gamble but, as Scratch himself had reminded him, if you hope to win you have to be in the game.

Chapter Nineteen

Angel opened the door to his office to find Billy fast asleep on the couch. He was covered entirely by his overcoat which rose and fell with each of his prodigious snores. Angel peeked under the coat to find Billy lying on his side, the office bottle of Fingal's Cave scotch tucked under one arm. It was, of course, empty.

Angel blamed himself. He'd been gone all afternoon and had neglected to give Billy anything to do. Without an assignment, Billy had found another, dependable way to spend his time.

Angel removed the bottle from under the elf's arm and placed it in the wastebasket. He'd tried to make as little noise as possible, but Billy stirred at the faint, metallic clink. A few seconds later, he rolled onto his back, opened his bleary eyes, and sighed softly. "You're back."

"I am."

Billy smacked his lips a couple of times and slurred out what sounded like "Thash nishe."

Angel frowned. "I see you've found something to occupy your time while I was gone."

Billy closed his eyes and a dreamy smile settled on his face. Seconds later, however, his eyes opened, snapped into focus, and he bolted up from the couch. "Geez, Boss," he said, shaking his shoulders like a rain-drenched puppy. "I completely forgot. You was gonna see Scratch today. How'd that go?"

Angel crossed the room to the file cabinet and the office coffee pot. Finding it empty, he replaced it and took a seat behind his desk. "It went surprisingly well. Scratch offered me my old job back."

"He what?" Billy sputtered.

Angel leaned back and tented his fingers. "I think he viewed Michael's coming to my rescue as a sign that the Archangelic Council is ready to…to reengage."

Billy scoffed. "Sure, they are. I'm guessin' they're ready to reengage with an old-fashioned, biblical-type ass whoopin'."

"I'm not sure the authors of the Bible ever referred to retribution as whooping ass."

"How about 'smite' then?"

"Better. Very *King James*. Although I don't necessarily think that Michael's visit means that Scratch and company are facing annihilation from on high. That's pretty much fallen out of style. I think there's a more subtle strategy in play."

Billy looked downcast. "So, no smiting then?"

"I fear not."

"Well, what's going on?"

The carriage clock on Angel's desk chimed. He stared at it a moment before answering. "In addition, I hope, to not wanting to see Balthasar and his goons hand me my rear end, I think Michael knew her appearance would alter the course of things. To make it appear that I might be a force to be reckoned with instead of an easily dismissible has-been."

Billy was aghast. "No one would ever think of you as a has-been, Boss. You're a…you're a—"

"A fallen angel with a drinking problem," Angel

146

interrupted. "You're just too kind to see it. But since her visit, my stock has risen. And I plan to take full advantage of it."

"I like the sound of that." Billy grinned. "So, what next, Boss?"

"My meeting with Scratch didn't yield much in the way of answers to the question of the missing Luther Deo, but it is clear that things are not at all what they seem."

"Like what?"

"Like what's going on at the Pole. And what really happened with Claus the Second? I'm beginning to doubt that his death was entirely reindeer related."

"But that does happen, Boss," Billy insisted. "There was that time a bunch of years back when Gustaf Criblecoblis—he worked for Kringle as a stable elf—he told his wife Pixie that he was going out to check on the alfalfa supply. Of course, he was really going out to meet up with Shiny Minstix who he'd been seeing on the sly. Anyway, they found him the next morning face down and stone dead in the reindeer muck. Ugly way to go. Funny thing. Later, Pixie and Shiny ended up real close, always together at Sweedlepipe's Ale House just laughing and free as a couple of wood snipes."

"Be that as it may," Angel said, "I find Claus the Second's death suspicious. I looked into it, and it doesn't appear that anyone outside the Company ever saw his body."

"No body?"

Angel nodded. "Oh, there was a memorial service, but no viewing. No casket at all. The news reports suggested that the body was just too mangled. They didn't want the last image of Father Christmas to be his mutilated corpse."

"But what about the cops? There had to be an investigation. There must be an official report."

Angel spread his hands before him and shook his head. "Yule Tide cops are well provided for by the Company. The police chief at the time of Claus the Second's death now heads security for them and brings in six figures."

"Okay, but what does Claus the Second's death got to do with elves at the Pole?"

"Maybe nothing. But suppose that they really are not being treated as well as reports would indicate? What if Claus the Second, at the time the world's most influential elf, took issue with this? What if he had to be silenced?"

"That would mean that Elvin—"

"It would mean that Elvin, now Santa, would definitely be on notice that actions have consequences."

Billy stared at Angel for a moment before plunking back down on the couch. Then he bent over and placed his head in his hands. Before long, he raised his head, his eyes deep and desolate. "You really think there's elves suffering at the Pole?"

Angel rose from his chair and went over to place a hand on Billy's shoulder. "I don't know, old friend. But we are going to have to find out."

"How do we do that?"

Angel removed his hand and shrugged. "I think we're going to have to head up to the Pole and see for ourselves."

"No way," Billy said, popping to his feet. "How could we? We can't just—"

"You let me worry about that," Angel told him.

Billy raised both eyebrows. "You know, Boss,

nothing makes me worry half as much as when you tell me not to worry."

Angel gave him a crooked smile. "I apologize. It might not come to that. In the meantime, let me map out our next steps. One thing I'm pretty sure of is that our best play is to keep shaking things up and see what rattles loose. I've already started. After I left Scratch, I went to see Noel Baba."

"Yeah? Why'd ya do that for?"

"Baba's in a tight spot. He says he wants to protect Gloria Deo. He definitely wants to protect what he's got going on with The Night Visitor, the ownership of which he owes to Scratch. And he certainly wants to be able to ride out any storms that might be on the horizon. So, I went to him and told him that Scratch had offered me my old job back."

"But you'd never take it."

"True. But Baba doesn't know that. I told him that Scratch wanted me back as a way to garner grace with the Archangelic Council. I told him that I was willing to appear to be Scratch's pawn while actually looking for a way to bring about his fall. I told him that the allegations about elfin mistreatment at the Pole have left Scratch vulnerable and my plan is to exploit that. I offered to protect him. If successful, I offered to cut him in."

"But if he owes everything to Scratch, wouldn't he go running to him to rat you out."

"He might. Or he might play things a little closer to the vest. See how things work out."

"But if he does tell Scratch your plan, aren't you screwed?"

"Maybe. But it's possible that Scratch might also choose to wait to see what develops. All I can do right now is to play everyone against each other. If Baba doesn't go to Scratch, he is being disloyal and that is something that we can use against him if necessary. If he does go to Scratch, he is only confirming what Scratch already knows, that I might try to make trouble for him. Before Michael's visit, this would have been of slight concern to him. But if he thinks I am now under divine protection, Scratch will have to be careful. For the moment, a partnership with me might seem the best strategy. For both of them."

"Cozying up to them two don't seem like the best idea, Boss. I remember a bedtime story my mother used to tell me. It had a bunny and a python. I can't remember all of the details but the moral? That I remember. The moral of the story was 'never trust a python who swears he just wants to cuddle.'"

Angel chuckled, reached out to the desk, and turned the clock to face him. "Well, it's been a long day. I'm ready for a nice meal and an early bedtime."

Billy grinned and thrust a hand into his pants pocket. "I got just the thing, Boss. If you're looking for carbs, I got a coupon for Joyeux Noodell. It's down on Panettone Street. Right where it crosses Linzer Way. Their biang biang noodles will knock you into the middle of next week."

"Sounds lovely, but—"

The office phone rang. Angel answered it and listened silently to the caller. "Of course," he said at last. "Tomorrow morning? Seven o'clock? It's a bit early, but if it's important I can be there. Thank you, Santa."

After Angel replaced the receiver, Billy approached the desk and hovered. "Well?" he asked. "That was Elvin?"

Angel nodded.

"What did he want?"

"He was a bit cagey about that. He asked me to come by the mansion tomorrow so we could talk about a matter of mutual interest." Angel paused. "Funny. He said that he wanted to make sure that my Christmas wishes come true."

"Okay," Billy said. "That is his job after all."

"True," Angel said, "but there was something about his tone that leads me to believe that he's not going to ask what to leave under my tree. There was a warning in his voice. I got the feeling he wanted to talk about whether I'd be around this Christmas at all."

Chapter Twenty

Fenster Dickens approached and set a mug of black coffee on the table in front of Angel. He then took a couple steps back and watched silently from a respectable distance. The Claus, sitting in the armchair opposite Angel, smiled and leaned forward. "Sorry to ask you around so early, Harry. You can't believe how busy we all are with Christmas approaching and this is the only time I had available."

"It's quite all right, I assure you."

"Thank you for being so accommodating." The Claus eyed Angel narrowly for a moment. "I wanted to talk to you about your investigation. I hear that there have been developments in your search for Luther. Congratulations."

Angel sipped some coffee. "I'm afraid you have been misinformed, Santa. I'm no closer now to discovering what happened to Luther Deo than I was when I took the case."

The Claus raised his eyebrows. "Really? Oh, that is unfortunate. We could certainly use him back on the job. It's only a few days until Christmas. There are so many details yet to be worked out. Luther was a wiz with the details." He paused. "Perhaps I'm wrong about this as well, but I've been told that you seem to be taking seriously those unsubstantiated rumors concerning how elves are treated at the Pole. In fact, I hope that I'm

152

mistaken. I can't see how the mendacities of a group of dangerous radicals could possibly help you find our logistics head."

Angel smiled. "I've found that when you are fumbling in the dark, it is unwise to discount anything you happen to bump into. You don't know if it is something that will lead you into the light or drag you further into darkness."

The Claus cast a glance at Dickens, then leaned back in his chair. Angel sipped more coffee. "Speaking of leading you into the light," the Claus began, "I also heard that you had a visit from a distinguished former colleague. Does that mean that you are near to returning to your former station?"

"Are you asking if I'm about to get my wings back?" Angel chuckled. "On that, Santa, your guess is as good as mine. But I will say that it seems to have raised my profile a bit. You've asked me around. Scratch deigned to see me. I'm assuming that you heard about that as well."

The Claus nodded. "I've always been very fond of you, Harry. You know that. Very protective of you. I am, of course, pleased that you are reconnecting with those for whom you formerly worked, both those supernal and otherwise, but our relationship was solid before that and will continue to be so no matter what changes, if any, are in the offing."

"That's very comforting, Santa."

The Claus peeked up at Dickens again before setting his eyes back on Angel. "I will say, however, that I'm not certain that our best interests lie in your pursuing information about elves at the Pole."

Angel raised an eyebrow. "*Our* best interests?"

"Yes. *Our* best interests. You see, Harry, we are all on the same page here. Aren't we, Mr. Dickens?"

Angel turned to Dickens who said nothing, his face as impassive as an ancient Roman bust.

"We've all heard the allegations," the Claus said, "and despite having been investigated and thoroughly discredited, the fact that they persist is…I guess you could say it is troubling. It is to me, anyway."

Angel peered over the rim of his mug, then set it on the table and stared.

"You see, Harry," the Claus continued, "when I accepted this position, I took on a huge responsibility. And it is not a responsibility that I take lightly. Once this Christmas is successfully in the books, I intend to look into the matter personally. I owe that to our former colleagues at the Pole. As the world's most recognizable elf, I must use my influence to help create the best possible lives for elves everywhere. Now, I hope and expect that allegations about Company inattentiveness toward those in retirement at the Pole is a misrepresentation by a group of bad actors who, for their own gain, are intent on impugning the reputation of those who safeguard Christmas. A false flag operation, if you will. But if there is even a shred of truth to what they are alleging, I will find it and expose it to scrutiny. Have no worry about that. But I think you will agree that this is something best handled by…Well, frankly, by elves. The allegations are being made by elves and must be repudiated by elves and not by others. Not by humans and, I'm afraid, not by other outsiders."

Angel smiled. "I wasn't always an outsider."

The Claus returned the smile. "Of course not. I didn't mean to imply that back when we were all together at the Pole you were anything but a cherished and welcome member of the community." His smile faded. "But as much as we embraced you, as proud as we were to have you in our midst, you must admit that you are, rather remarkably, something other than an elf."

Angel let his eyes wander around the room, the roaring fire, the paintings on the wall, the odd mix of elf and human-sized furniture. He sighed deeply. "You may very well be right," he said at last. "The elfin population of the world rightly looks to you for leadership. For protection." He paused. "That was true in Kringle's time and I'm sure it was also true of your predecessor, Claus the Second. It's a pity that he passed after such a short time. I've heard he was the very definition of a good elf."

A cloud passed over the Claus's expression but quickly dissipated. "Yes. He was very deserving of the position. We lost him far too soon."

"Hmm," Angel hummed. "Do you know if he was aware of what was being said about mistreatment of retirees at the Pole? Was that something he was looking into before his death?"

Fenster Dickens stepped forward. "I don't believe those rumors were extant at the time."

It was the first time that Angel had heard Dickens speak. His voice was a bit on the high side but had a hard edge. Not brittle. Rather forged like a well-made blade.

"Not extant?" Angel asked. "You mean that they hadn't yet been made public?"

Dickens's eyes widened revealing a spark. Either anger or interest. Angel could not be certain which. "I don't believe that such allegations had been made at the time," Dickens clarified.

"I see," Angel said.

"*Do* you?" the Claus asked. "Do you see how your continued inquiries into this matter could interfere with ours? If the rumors are true, and I'm not saying that they are, but if they were, those responsible would do everything they could to keep that truth from coming out. It could…It could put elves in danger. I simply cannot allow that."

A corner of Angel's mouth curled. "Nor could I, Santa," he said. "Nor could I. And while I have an obligation to continue to look for Luther Deo, I see now that I have perhaps an even greater obligation to refrain from any actions that might endanger those with whom I worked so long and so well."

"I'm so glad to hear that," the Claus said, smiling brightly and rising from his chair. "As I said, dear boy, I have only your best interests in mind. It's not just elves that I worry about. As recent events have shown, pursuing secrets can put anyone in danger. Even you. I mean, if your empyreal colleague had not come to your aid when those ruffians apprehended you the other morning, things could have ended very differently."

Angel stood and shook the Claus's outstretched hand. "It is indeed heartwarming to know that you hold my welfare in such regard. Thank you, Santa."

As he turned to the door, Angel met Dickens's eyes. The spark was still there. Interest, not anger, he decided.

As Angel made his way to his parking space, his cellphone rang. It was Billy.

"You're up early," Angel said.

"You got that right. And don't expect me to make a habit of it. But I had to know. How'd you survive your meeting with his nibs?"

"It was very enlightening. He was quite adamant

about one thing. He'd like us to stick to looking for Luther Deo, but he'd prefer that we leave rumors about Company impropriety to him and his team. He also seemed quite concerned about my well-being. He even called me 'dear boy.'"

"Wait a minute," Billy cautioned. "Ain't that what Scratch keeps calling you?"

"It is."

"That ain't good, Boss."

"No," Angel agreed. "But it is enlightening."

"That business about Company impro…improprierty? Does that mean he wants you to lay off looking into bad things happening to elves at the Pole?

"It does."

"What did you tell him?" Billy asked, anger seeping into his voice.

"I told him I would."

"But…but…but—"

"Calm down, Billy. I didn't mean it."

"You mean you lied to Santa Claus?"

"Yes. That's what I mean. It's not like the jolly old elf shouldn't be expecting it. Every kid that's ever crawled into his lap and told him how good they'd been that year is, in some respect, lying to him. Just ask their parents."

"I guess you're right, Boss," Billy said, "but them kids are in his lap for a minute. You gotta live in this town. Yule Tide is all about the Claus. Him and the ones he answers to. It ain't healthy to get too far on their bad side."

"That's true," Angel agreed. "But on this road we find ourselves…Well, I'm afraid there is a risk that my prognosis could turn decidedly negative."

Billy sighed. "Let's do what we can to make sure you don't flatline all together."

Chapter Twenty-One

Angel got to the office at about eight-thirty, well before the other tenants were in, and found Gabriel Morningstar waiting for him. He slumped against the office door in the dimly lit hallway. His work tuxedo and cummerbund bore a two-toned look due to the bright red material being soaked through with blood. More blood had pooled beneath him.

At first, Angel thought the elf was dead, but on closer look saw a gentle rising of his chest—just before Morningstar let out a muted moan. Angel was afraid to touch him but, in a voice as soft as the whisper of eternity, the elf said, "Help me in."

Angel unlocked the office and carried the elf inside, laying him on the couch. Morningstar's right arm slipped off the cushions toward the floor revealing a small envelope grasped in his hand. Its manilla surface was smeared with more blood. Angel carefully placed Morningstar's arm back on the couch.

The elf managed a slight smile. "They found out and shot me. Outside the club. They ran," he said with slow deliberation. "Left me there. They didn't know I ... They didn't know I had this." He raised a feeble arm, handing the bloody envelope to Angel.

As Angel took it from him, Morningstar coughed. A trickle of blood flowed from the corner of his mouth. "I hope you are who you say you are," he said. Then he coughed once again and breathed no more.

Angel unsealed the envelope and peeked inside. He then crossed to his desk, picked up the phone, and dialed Billy. "I gotta see you. Now."

"I can come right into work, Boss. Jeez, I shoulda been there before this but I got stuck doing an online crossword. Say, what's a ten-letter word for Christmas tree? Ends in an 'm.'"

"The office is no good,' Angel told him. "Going to have to be your place."

Billy took a moment to reply. "What's wrong?"

"Unfortunately, our office is now a crime scene. It will be anyway once the cops get wind of what happened. Do you have a computer with a CD drive?"

"You know I do. I got one of everything. But what's this about a crime scene?"

Angel ignored the question. "There's a disc we need to check out."

Billy lowered his voice. "We're not gonna listen to Andy Williams, are we?"

"I'll be right over," Angel said.

Billy lived in a single room occupancy building in downtown Yule Tide. It was a hundred-year-old former hotel that had lost any pretense of glamour. Its red brick façade had faded beneath a layer of moss and mildew. Many of the original rooms, which had been small enough to begin with, were further subdivided to serve as housing for indigent elves who, it was said, needed far less room than real people.

Angel usually preferred to meet with Billy in their far more spacious office and had visited his room on only a couple of previous occasions. Still, it was as he remembered it. A bench against one wall was topped with a thin foam cushion and covered by a threadbare quilt that Billy had once said belonged to his mother. A pillow cased in a flower print was propped on one end. A plastic chair, evidently elementary-school surplus, was the only other seating option. It was placed at the center of a sturdy table directly opposite a notebook computer connected by a cable to an old dot matrix printer. Nearly every other square inch of the table and most of the floor was littered with electronic devices. There were CRT monitors, piles of hard drives, disc drives, several old desktop computer towers—many with their covers removed revealing their circuit-board insides like those cutaway anatomical models found in doctors' offices. An oscilloscope bathed the room in flickering, green light.

When Angel held out the envelope, Billy stared first at it, then at his employer. After taking the envelope with just the tips of his fingers, Billy said, "Bathroom's down the hall, Boss. You might want to wash up." He raised the blood-smeared envelope. "You got a little of this on your suit."

Angel nodded. "The disc is in the envelope," he said. "We need to see what's on it. Get started without me. I'll only be a minute."

Angel was surprised to find the shared bathroom empty. With so many elves living on each floor, he had to wonder how long the line for the bathroom normally was in the morning.

Returning to Billy's room, Angel found his friend sitting at the table, peering intently at the screen. The empty envelope rested beside the laptop. "It's an audio file, Boss." Billy told him. Then he turned around, his eyes glinting with anxiety. "You said the office is crime scene? You wanna tell me more about that?"

Angel took a seat on the bench that doubled as Billy's bed. "After I left the mansion, I went to the office. That elf I told you about? Gabriel Morningstar? The men's room attendant at The Night Visitor? He was there. He was shot. Gut shot. He handed me that envelope and died. His body's still there. Only a matter of time before it's discovered."

Billy sighed. "Someone shot him at our office?"

Angel shook his head. "No. Morningstar said he was shot outside the club."

"Jeez, Boss, that's clear across town!"

Angel nodded. "Morningstar must have been pretty tough to make as far as he did, as wounded as he was. Whatever's on that disc was important enough to him to die for. I need to hear that audio file before his death draws attention."

"No problem, Boss." Billy turned back to the computer and clicked on the touchpad. The small room swelled with sound. He toggled the volume down and he and Angel listened together.

The recording was a bit muffled, as though the microphone had been hidden. But the voices were clear enough. It took Angel a moment to recognize the first voice. The promotional video, he realized at last. The interview with Luther Deo. And unlike the smooth professionalism he'd shown in the video, this time Luther was obviously upset.

"It's simply unconscionable," he said. "I didn't believe what they were saying for a minute. But then I went up there myself and I saw—"

Scratch's calm, funereal voice cut him off. "What you saw, dear Luther, is open to interpretation."

"Interpretation?" Luther Deo countered. "Elves have died. And from what I can see, they died needlessly. And for what? The Company's bottom line? What is the life of a single elf worth? And we are talking about hundreds. Perhaps thousands."

"Don't be such an alarmist, Luther," Scratch said. "I know what you witnessed looks bad but only from the point of view of those who wish us harm. Everything that lives eventually dies. Who is to say what caused the deaths of these elves you are talking about? Many were elderly. Many were in ill health. Death is a natural part of life. Are you blaming the Company for something that is inevitable? Even ordained?"

"Dammit, Scratch. I talked to their families. I heard about the constant shortages. I've seen those hovels you call a retirement village. I wouldn't kennel my dog in one of them."

Scratch laughed, more cackle than laugh. "Well, you've always been more attached to your dog than most."

"We are not talking about my dog!" Deo shouted. "We are talking about elfin lives. The lives of elves, some of whom worked for Kringle for hundreds of years. Elves who were promised security and safety. Elves that you, Mr. Scratch, have betrayed."

Another voice sounded on the recording. Elvin's voice. "Now, now, Luther," he said. "We have been made aware that certain subcontractors may have been cutting corners, but nothing that would result in what you are talking about. And whatever shortcomings that have been discovered are being addressed. Solutions are being implemented. Rest assured of that."

Deo's voice calmed. "The problem, Santa, is that I

don't believe you."

"You think I would lie to you, Luther?" Elvin asked, a sob rising in his voice.

"I don't know," Deo admitted. "But I've been up there. You haven't. You haven't visited the Pole since the Company moved the operation. You may not be lying. You may just be ignorant of the truth. But Scratch and the Board? It's inconceivable that they don't know. This is more than 'cutting corners.' This is deliberate neglect. Criminal neglect. And I intend to see those responsible pay a price."

"You're distressed, Luther," Elvin said. "That's perfectly understandable. We are, all of us, distressed. This is a distressing situation. But it is one that is already in hand. Believe me, steps are being taken. Changes are being made. Improvements. Things are changing for the better. Let us handle this in house. You are the one who has brought this to our attention. You are the one who made the trip to the Pole. And you can be at the head of the team that will make things right. You've only to trust us. Trust the Company. Trust me. Trust Mr. Scratch."

The recording went quiet. Billy turned up the volume, but for several seconds it was as if the recording had ended. Then Deo's voice came through strong and determined.

"I'm not you, Santa," he said. "I can't be lied to about the most important things. I can't have my trust betrayed. I can't see lives destroyed by greed and indifference and remain silent. I can't simply trust that this…this Mr. Scratch will do anything besides what he has always done. Lie. Hide the truth. Manipulate the media. Manufacture goodwill where none is warranted. Allow those in his care to suffer and die and all to line his pockets and those of his cronies. No, Santa. I am not like you. I cannot and will not stand idly by while those in our care suffer the worst kind of neglect."

"And what is it that you proposed to do?"" Scratch's voice returned. His tone was flat, even disinterested.

"I have documentation, Mr. Scratch," Deo said, his voice stiffening with resolve. "I have proof that what you have been telling the world about the Pole is nothing but self-serving reindeer dung. Manufactured and disseminated by a compliant press. But there are media outlets that you do not control. I will take this documentation and my testimony to them. I will do so this very day."

"Oh, my," Scratch said. "That would bring up a number of questions. Not the least of those concerning your complicity."

"My complicity? Just what is that supposed to mean?"

"It's just that I seem to recall a conversation some weeks ago when we discussed this very issue. At the time you were keen to launch a further inquiry but as I remember you lost interest when I suggested that you had enough on your hands and that I was, in fact, planning on giving you a rather substantial bonus for...How did we put it at the time? For focusing your considerable talents on the logistical challenges the Company faces during our runup to Christmas to the exception of other concerns. As I recall, you readily accepted that bonus. One hundred thousand dollars. A tidy sum."

"Are you saying that I accepted a bride?"

"Oh, my dear, no. Not at all. But if you take your rather fanciful story to the press, I don't see how I can stop others from thinking so."

"I'll give the money back."

"Splendid, dear Luther," Scratch said. "Just splendid. You do that. I'm sure that will remove all suspicion from your good name. Be my guest. And more than that, take your so-called truth to those bastions of journalistic integrity of which you speak. Go ahead. Place a black mark on Christmas just weeks before the kiddoes of the world expect a visit from Santa. Foul the dreams of youngsters the world round. Their loss will be your gain. You'll be a hero. A man of integrity. Think of the reputation you will garner. Never mind the disappointment of millions of youngsters."

"As if you really care about them," Deo said.

Scratch ignored him. "You will, of course, lose your position here at the Company, but what matter? With your newfound hero status, I'm sure that you'll find a way to survive economically. Of course, there will be those that will see your actions as little more than the fabrications of a disgruntled former employee. And one of dubious character at that. But again, small concern to someone of your innate integrity."

The recording once again fell silent save for what sounded like light drumming. Fingernails against a desktop perhaps. Then Scratch's voice returned, flinty and arrogant. "But what of the lovely Mrs. Deo? I do hope that she has not become too attached to the lifestyle that our generous compensation has made possible. I would hate to see her running back to the crowd she used to associate with. It was so noble of you to have rescued her from that life among those disreputable figures. The underworld is a harsh place. It can shrivel the bloom of even the most radiant flower."

"I'm warning you, Scratch!" Deo thundered. "Leave my wife out of this."

"Oh, my dear sir," Scratch answered. "I am not bringing her into anything. I fear that blame will lie entirely with you."

There was a pause, then Deo said, "You can go to hell, Mr. Scratch."

Scratch chortled. "Hell is something I know far more about than you, dear Luther. Perhaps this will illustrate what I mean. Come closer. Come closer to the desk. I think you will find this most illuminating."

After a moment there was a sound on the recording. Angel couldn't quite place it. The sound of something creaking open. Something ancient. Like a shriek from far off carried on the wind. Then there was a strangled gasp, and a thud as though whatever had opened had fallen closed. Then silence.

After a moment, Elvin's shaky voice was heard.

"Jesus, Scratch. Was that necessary?"

"Necessary? Yes," Scratch assured him. "And let's be clear. Jesus had nothing to do with it."

Chapter Twenty-Two

The cargo sleigh had been loaded in the full light of day, but the evening's shadows had gathered before the crew arrived with the reindeer. It was a big load. It would take all eight to get the sleigh to its destination. The reindeer were large, dwarfing the elves that led them to the sleigh. Judging from the size and number of points on their antlers, these were mature, experienced fliers. The lead reindeer chuffed loudly as it was being harnessed. The elf tending it laid a calming hand on the bridge of the animal's nose and murmured softly.

Thanks to the timetable provided by Doc Praetorius, Angel and Billy had managed to get aboard the sleigh only moments before the crew arrived with the reindeer. Angel peered out from behind the cases of tinned vegetables and boxes of sanitary products that they had snugged behind. Watching and waiting for the sleigh driver to take his seat.

Praetorius had assured them that the interior of the sleigh was both pressurized and climate-controlled, but Billy had made sure to wear both a pair of fur-lined boots and a down parka over his uniform just in case.

The day had flown by. After listening to the recording, Angel had called Praetorius, asking him when the next cargo sleigh was scheduled to fly to the Pole. He'd have to hurry. The next flight was that very evening.

Stealing a ride to the Pole was not high on Billy's wish list. Instead, he insisted that they take the recording to the authorities. It was, he maintained, proof enough to warrant not only a redirected investigation of Luther Deo's disappearance, but also of Company malfeasance. "This is the straight stuff, Boss," Billy said. "We've got 'em by the short hairs."

Angel had to set him straight. He'd listened to it twice and there was nothing damning on the recording. Neither Scratch nor Elvin had admitted any wrongdoing. Quite the contrary. They had insisted that the Company was doing everything they could to right any wrongs— real or imagined. And that creaking and thud they'd heard? That could have been a cabinet opening and closing. Or even the door to the office as Luther Deo made an abrupt exit. The stifled cry? It might have been a sneeze. Everything on the recording was easily dismissible. Nothing that could be tied directly to Deo's disappearance.

No. If they were going to pin anything on Scratch and Company, Angel and Billy would need real proof. And the only place to get it was at the Pole.

Both Angel and Billy knew from experience that travel by sleigh is not for the faint of heart. The reindeer are harnessed and then tethered to the sleigh using a system of rigging that allows them to pull the load and, once free from the ground, the sleigh is supposed to become relatively stable behind them. But it is subject to both turbulence and the whims of the, at times, recalcitrant reindeer. It can be a very bumpy ride.

"I can go alone," Angel had insisted.

Billy stared. He shuddered briefly as though taken by a sudden chill. He breathed heavily several times through his nose, then closed his eyes, and held his breath as though tamping down something waxing within him. "I'm with you, Boss," he said at last.

Angel nodded, pulled out his cell phone, and called Gloria Deo.

He was not terribly forthcoming, telling her only that he would be gone until the next day, that there were no new developments, but that he was hopeful he'd have something more to report soon.

"There's something you're not telling me," she said. It was not a question.

"I'll be in touch," Angel told her.

After a pause, Mrs. Deo said, "Be careful. I wouldn't want to lose you, too."

Angel held on to the receiver for several moments after Mrs. Deo clicked off the call. Her comment left him feeling hollow. As though something deep inside him, something important, was missing.

The sleigh driver arrived, opened the door to the cab and climbed aboard, jostling the load. As he did, the contents of several large, sealed, gray tubs aboard the sleigh sloshed within them. Angel ducked back into his hiding place and heard Billy sigh beside him. Either a sigh or a sob, Angel wasn't sure which. He reached over and placed a reassuring hand on Billy's shoulder.

After a few moments, the reins snapped, hooves pawed the ground, and the sleigh lurched forward. Gaining speed, it lifted into the sky.

Had it a place to land, an airplane flight from Yule Tide to the North Pole would take some four hours. By sleigh it is much shorter. Angel anticipated less than an hour. It's one of the advantages of magic.

Angel was grateful for the short duration of the

flight as stretches of calm were punctuated by intervals where the sleigh would wobble and pitch wildly, not unlike running white water rapids in a dollar-store inner tube. Both he and Billy were relieved when the sleigh touched safely down on the field just outside the North Pole complex.

Once on the ground, Angel again peered out from his hiding place and watched as the sleigh driver maneuvered his load through the gates and into complex. There was a whoosh as the gates closed behind them sealing off the controlled environment of the campus from the extreme cold and corrosive winds outside.

The sleigh made its way toward a warehouse located less than a mile from what used to be known as Santa's village. A Company crew would be waiting inside the warehouse to unload the sleigh. Unless they exited the vehicle before it got inside, Angel and Billy would be discovered.

"Time to move," Angel said.

Slipping from his recess among the boxes, Angel crawled toward the rear of the sleigh, Billy trailing him. Doc Praetorius had told him of an access panel that would be found there. It took some time, but Angel finally spotted it. Four knobs at the corners secured it to the aft skin of the sleigh. Angel opened the panel just as the sleigh was pulling into the warehouse. Angel jumped first. Used to landings from his winged days, he alighted gracefully. Billy much less so. Picking himself up from the ground, Billy joined Angel as both hurried around the corner of the building and out of sight.

They began the walk to the village proper under a starlit sky. Angel had never quite understood the magic that enabled the campus to be both open to the sky yet secure from the frigid temperatures of the Arctic. In the past, he'd just appreciated the warmth. But now it seemed much colder than he remembered. Perhaps, he thought, that magic was on the wane.

It would take only ten minutes to reach the village, but every moment would count as Praetorius had told them that the supply sleigh would make its return run to Yule Tide after only four hours. They would have to get the proof they were looking for and get back to the sleigh within that timeframe or they would be stranded at the Pole for two weeks. Angel set a pace that Billy's shorter legs could barely match.

Memories flooded Angel as he made his way down the streets of Santa's village. At first, things seemed as they had always been. Small houses with cedar shake roofs and double-hung windows fronted the boulevard that led to the old Santa's workshop. Many were trimmed with fanciful curlicues and cutouts of Christmas trees and snowflakes. But only meager light shined through most of those windows. Some were completely dark. And the streets were empty. In Kringle's time, this was a village of more than one hundred thousand elves, bustling with activity. But here it was early evening, a time when these streets used to be thronging with elves coming home from the workshop, others going out for an evening's entertainment, still others taking the air as they walked their dogs or strolled with their babies. The now deserted village struck Angel as eerily familiar. Like the deadening stillness he'd encountered long ago as he walked through a once thriving hamlet in a Europe gripped by the Great Plague.

At the end of the main boulevard, they reached the workshop. Angel remembered it well. Single-storied and about 25,000 square feet, the building had been fashioned from hand-hewn beams and planks and topped with a cedar shake roof. Built to withstand the North Pole climate, it had been constructed centuries ago—long before the village and its environs had been sealed. The workshop had always been scrupulously maintained by a team of dedicated carpenter elves—its exterior regularly stained, weathered roof shakes replaced, its windows wiped so often and so clear that it would appear as if they had not been fitted with glass.

But that was before the move to Yule Tide. The workshop that stood before them was in disrepair—its siding faded, pieces of the roof missing, the windows clouded with grime.

No light shone from within, and the only sound Angel could clearly make out was a faint creaking as the ancient structure settled. The front double doors were securely locked, so Angel and Billy made their way around to the rear of the workshop. The back door was also locked but checking each window, Angel was able to find one whose frame had rotted. He pulled a Leatherman multitool from his pocket and began chipping at the rot-softened wood. Before long he'd managed to pry open the clasp securing the window. He then planted his feet, and pushed upward, screeching the window open. He boosted Billy inside and the elf unlocked the door allowing Angel to enter.

Angel pulled a small flashlight from his coat pocket. The beam revealed the old workbenches still surrounding the long oval conveyer belt that had once been the toy line. Tools of every kind hung from wooden pegs fixed to the walls. Mallets, awls, and hand saws, all at the ready but no workers' hands to reach for them. A half dozen looms stood sentry on one side of the space, one still warped and waiting vainly for the touch of the weaver. And above it all, cantilevered and overlooking the floor of the workshop, was the office from which Kringle had directed the operation.

Angel climbed the stairs to the office and stepped inside to look out through the wide windows and survey the scene—once so lively, now a void, still and silent, as though all that had once been there, everything that had once happened there, had passed from existence leaving only traces as intangible yet enduring as memory.

As Angel descended the stairs, he heard something. A gentle scuttling along one wall. He directed the beam of his flashlight toward the sound and caught just a glimpse of a rodent—small, a mouse or tundra vole—skirting along the baseboard.

Back at Billy's side, Angel said, "It doesn't look like there's anything for us here. We'll need to look elsewhere if we hope to get what we came for."

Billy nodded and led the way back outside. Once there, Angel hesitated, glancing first back toward the village where only an occasional light shone dimly from the cottages, then into the darkness that lay beyond the workshop. Which direction, he wondered, would yield the results they sought? He needed witnesses. Statements. Evidence. But where to get it? Although he believed that it is in darkness that one finds secrets, he turned back toward the faint light of the village.

Billy fell in behind him, but before they got far, Angel thought he heard footsteps. Not the scurrying of a rodent. No. Something distinctly larger. Pressing a finger to his lips, he directed the elf toward the back of the workshop. Once there, the pair pressed their backs against the building and into shadow, trying to make themselves as small and unseen as possible. Then they waited.

They heard nothing. Angel wondered if he might be imagining things. Sometimes, he thought, you want something so bad your mind provides it. He turned to Billy and offered him a defeated smile.

Then, there it was again. The sound of footsteps. This time clearer. Stronger. Someone was approaching.

It was difficult to make out the figure in the dim light. Judging from its size, it was an elf. Hunched over, the elf came slowly, each step weighted, uncertain. When the elf had nearly reached them, Angel stepped away from the building.

It was a female, wrapped in a thick cloak that made her appear quite wide, even corpulent. She wore a woolen kerchief on her head—red, green, and white. Christmas colors, Angel thought. Hers was an aged, heavily lined face with pale blue eyes squinting out from among the wrinkles, her wizened cheeks glowing pink in the cold.

"Excuse me," Angel said softly.

He might as well have set off a blasting cap. Hearing him, the elf jerked to full height and let out a shriek that tore through the landscape like a fissure from a sudden earthquake.

Angel held up both hands. "I am sorry," he said, careful to keep his voice down. "I didn't mean to scare you."

The expression on the elf's face went from fright to puzzlement and then right on to indignation.

"Didn't mean to scare me?" she snapped. "Just what did you mean then? Sneakin' up on your elders?

You…You popinjay. You just about gave me a heart attack."

"I didn't mean—"

"You said that already. Just 'cause I'm old doesn't mean you have to go around repeatin' yourself."

"I'm sorry, but—"

"There you go again. You think I'm deaf. I tell you, just 'cause someone hits the ripe old age of eight hundred doesn't mean they're ready for the bone yard." She pulled a skinny arm out from under the cloak she had wrapped around her and waggled an irate finger at Angel.

"I need your help," Angel implored her. "You see, my colleague and I are—"

The finger she pointed at Angel curled into a fist. "You're gonna need my help all right," the elf snarled. "You're gonna need my help gettin' back up after I knock you on your ass."

"I, uh…I, uh…" Angel stammered.

Billy stepped away from the building and approached the infuriated elf. Peering closely at her, at last a bright smile flashed across his face. "Cecily?" he asked. "Cecily Zagnutt?"

Wheeling on Billy and still shaking her fist, she said, "What's it to you, Bub? You want a piece of this?"

"Cecily. Don't you recognize me? It's me. Billy. Billy Goodman."

She shook her head violently. "Can't be. Billy Goodman lit out of here years ago. Probably the only truly intelligent thing that pie-eyed skylarker ever did. Billy never was one to—" Cecily paused abruptly and stepped forward until she was nearly nose-to-nose with Billy. Scanning his face she said, "There is some resemblance, though, I'll warrant that. Only that schnozzle of yours. Too pulpy, if you ask me."

A beaming, Billy turned to Angel. "I know her, Boss. Cecily and I used to…Back in the day, we used to, you know, go out walking together. She was Cecily Razzlemuffin back then." He turned back to the female elf and shook his head dolefully. "I lost her to my old pal Gimbel Zagnutt. The backstabbing son-of-a-fruitcake-vendor. I remember the time—"

Cecily took a step back and flung both arms skyward. "Well, poke me in the eye and call me Blinky! It *is* you! Billy Goodman, as I live and breathe!" Then she rushed forward and throwing both arms wide, wrapped Billy in a tight embrace. Billy didn't have time to even raise his arms before being pinned by Cecily's hug, but nonetheless managed to maintain a strained grin.

When, at last, she let go, Billy reached out a hand and brushed Cecily's cheek with his fingertips. "It's been too long, Ducks," he said. Then, pointing toward Angel, he said, "This is Harry. He's my boss. We're here to—"

"No use telling me, Billy," Cecily interrupted, glowering at Harry, her face screwed up with disgust. "One thing I've learned from these last years is that nothin' good can come from associatin' with their kind. I tell you, Billy. You can't trust 'em."

"But Harry's not—"

Cecily put both palms over her ears. "I don't want to hear it. They're devils, Billy. All of 'em. Devils. Every. One. And I'll tell you another thing. If I find out they let humans into heaven, you can write me a ticket to the other place. Don't want nothin' to do with any of 'em."

"Funny you should mention heaven, Mrs. Zagnutt," Angel said.

"That's right, Cecily," Billy said. "Harry here's not actually human. I mean, he looks human, but he's really—"

"What kind of folderol are you slingin' here, Billy? I know a human when I see one and while I admit this one's better lookin' than most, that don't mean—"

"Cecily. You got to listen to me," Billy interrupted. "This here is no ordinary guy. This is Harry, um, *Harold* Angel. You might remember him. He used to work with the Claus. Not any of them new ones either. The boss here used to work with Kringle. The elf himself."

Cecily shook her head. "I met that Harold Angel once. Years ago. At a retirement party for Flora Pennywort. Flora's passed on now, but this was before. That Harold Angel was tall like this fellow, but he had somethin' this fellow don't have. Wings. Magnificent, white feathered wings. If this fellow is that fellow, then where's his wings?"

"About that," Billy began.

Angel raised both palms helplessly. "I lost my wings, Mrs. Zagnutt," he said. "Like you, I was lied to. After Kringle died, it seemed like all was lost. Then the Company came in and it seemed like hope restored. I believed them when they said they could save Christmas. That they'd keep things as they were. Even when I was shown proof that they were not what they seemed, I couldn't give up the hope. Even when I was recalled, even when they told me what I would lose by refusing to leave the village, I stayed. I even followed them on to Yule Tide. Like a fool, I thought I could make a difference."

Angel paused and stared off toward the village, at the few lights flickering there like the last embers of a spent Yule log.

"I failed, Mrs. Zagnutt," Angel continued. "I failed you. I failed myself. I failed us all. What Billy says is true. I'm not a human. But I'm no longer an angel either. I'm not much of anything anymore. I'm just a being in search of redemption. In search of a way forward."

Cecily stepped toward Angel, peering up at him, bringing her face as close to his as she could. Angel stooped slightly to make it easier for her to study him. As he did, Angel realized that he'd seen this elf before. She was the elf from the news accounts of the delegation to the Pole. The accounts that had exonerated the Company. The elf whose single, grateful tear absolved them in the public mind of all wrongdoing.

After a few moments of mutual examination, recognition sparked in Cecily's eyes, and she broke into a wide smile. "Well, roll me in cocoa powder and call me Truffles," she said. "You just might be that Harold Angel after all."

"Cecily," Billy said, "we don't have a lot of time. We need to document what's going on here. How elves are treated. We need to show the world. And to do that, we need your help."

Cecily waved a dismissive hand. "That's been tried before. Didn't change nothin'. If anythin', it made things worse. The truth don't mean bupkis no more."

"But we gotta try," Billy insisted.

Cecily stared at him for some time. At first, her eyes glinted with mistrust, but they softened into something that looked more like resolve. She reached toward Billy and lightly brushed his cheek with her outstretched fingers. "Can't say as I'm not tired of tryin'," she said. "Can't say as I'm not now one for givin' up. But I'll see what I can do to help you. That I'll do. Just don't be askin' me to hope. That I gave up long ago."

Chapter Twenty-Three

Except for a single candle, the interior of the small home that Cecily led them to was dark. And cold.

"Sorry,' she said. "Electricity is out. They call it a rollin' blackout, but it done rolled over us and stayed there. We ain't had no lights since I don't even remember when."

"There seemed to be plenty of electricity back at the warehouse where they unload the cargo sleigh," Angel observed.

"There would be, wouldn't there," Cecily said.

The house was small, clean, and crowded with elf-sized furniture. In the living room, twin sofas faced each other across a low, rectangular table, and the back of an easy chair in the corner was covered with a crocheted afghan of sapphire blue and rose. An open kitchen featured a black iron, wood-burning cookstove and a small table with two chairs. The open shelving above the stove was mostly empty. Angel spotted a can of beef stew and some tinned salmon, but otherwise the cupboard appeared bare. Near the table, a doll-sized silver tea service peeked out from the glass doors of a china closet.

"I'd make you a cuppa," Cecily told them, "but there ain't been tea since last Christmas. And no wood for a fire for a month or longer."

"That's all right, Ducks," Billy said. "Neither Harry

nor me are big tea drinkers." Taking a long look around he said, "I...um...I don't see Gimbel. I'm still a bit sore he stole you away from me but, heck, I guess that was centuries ago. I like to see him if he's around."

Cecily shook her head. "Sorry, Billy. We lost poor Gimbel. Last year. He got the ague. There weren't no medicine. No doctors. He just shivered and shivered. Couldn't keep anythin' down. One mornin' he just died."

Cecily wiped something from her eye. "Not sure it was even the ague that got him. After a while he just lost hope. Didn't see no better nothin' comin' for him. For us." She paused to glance around the room. "An elf that don't got nothin' to live for just naturally stops livin'."

Billy sighed but made no further reply.

"Would you consent to an interview, Mrs. Zagnutt?" Angel asked. "We'd like to document the privations that you and the other retired elves have been experiencing here."

"*Retired* elves?" Cecily asked. "Is that what they're callin' it now? Shut down the workshop? Try to drive us from our homes? Starve us out? And they're callin' that retirement?"

"Billy brought a small video camera," Angel said. "If we could get you on videotape?"

"Been there, done that, Angelface," Cecily said. "Ain't nobody gonna believe a thing I say after what I told them the last time they was here."

"About that," Angel said. "I have seen the interview you gave to that press contingent that the Company brought up here last year. I'm assuming you were coerced into making the statements that you did."

"It weren't no interview, and it weren't no contingent," Cecily insisted. "It was just a couple of guys with a pile of cameras and such. Them and these three hateful assholes they brought along to threaten us. I was with my granddaughter that day. They grabbed us off the street, propped me up, and told me what to say. When I told 'em where they could shove it, one of 'em—this short, wide troll with a unibrow—snatches up me little darlin'. Her all bawlin' and this prick holds her upside down by her ankles and threatens to bleed right there and roast her like a pig. He'd a done it, too. That's all we are to them humans. Livestock." Cecily paused. "Yeah, Angelpuss. You could say I was coerced."

"I'm afraid we haven't much time, Mrs. Zagnutt," Angel said. "We have a sleigh to catch. If you're willing, Billy will set up his equipment and you can tell us the real story."

Cecily nodded. "If you think it will do any good."

Billy's equipment consisted of a brick-sized, hand-held digital camcorder. Angel was surprised. It had been a long time since he'd seen one.

During the interview, Angel asked a few questions, but mostly allowed Cecily to tell her story in her own way. She talked about the shock of losing Kringle, how the whole village mourned. Of their fear for the future and their joy when the Company arrived and appeared ready to keep doing things the Kris Kringle way. How thrilled they were with the election of Claus the Second, an elf they all knew and trusted. But then she related how everything changed. The Company announced that they were closing the workshop—a place that had been the center of their lives for centuries. There would be a new Santa's village, they were told, to be built in a new town in a new place. "What was wrong with the old one?" Cecily wanted to know. Then they were told that only a small number of elves would be needed in the new place. That most of them would no longer be doing the work they had done for the equivalent of dozens of human lifetimes. But they were assured that those left behind would be well cared for. A luxurious retirement condominium complex would be built. With tennis courts, pools, and fine restaurants. Those who wished to stay in their homes were welcome to, but the new complex, to be dubbed Shady Glen, would be a resort. Every day would be like a vacation. There would now be time to relax, to enjoy family and friends, to savor a well-earned retirement.

Then she recounted what really happened after the move. How all services to the homes in the village became unreliable. Garbage left to pile up. The clinic closed. Food shortages prompting long lines for insufficient and unpalatable foodstuffs—gray and foul-smelling meat, vegetables shriveled and slimy. Meanwhile those who had moved into the promised retirement complex were no longer seen in the village at all. Visitors were not allowed, the grounds patrolled by armed, uniformed guards. But stories emerged. Of how the much-touted Shady Glen was little more than a bunkhouse, a prison, a warehouse where elves were crowded together and left to fend for themselves.

Angel asked her about the interview, about how she had praised the Company for keeping their promises, for giving them the rich retirement they deserved. Her anger was palpable, but she held it together. She repeated the story of how she was forced to read their statement, how the tear that fell so poignantly down her cheek was from fear for her granddaughter and her utter helplessness.

Then she related how the sickness came. They called

it the ague. It was worst for those in the bunkhouse. Elf to elf it spread. Hundreds died. So many that a fleet of trucks formed a constant line of traffic hauling corpses from Shady Glen to a place beyond the rear perimeter of the North Pole complex. But it wasn't just Shady Glen. The ague swept through the village as well. Elves young and old, their small bodies lifeless and loaded like so much refuse for transport to the mass grave that had been dug to accommodate them. When Gimbel passed, his body too was loaded up to be hauled away. Cecily had begged them to let her accompany him. To let her say some words over where he would be laid to rest. They refused. But Cecily Zagnutt would not be denied. She waited until nightfall and followed the tracks of the trucks that she'd heard the drivers refer to as "cadaver wagons." She knew how to get past the rear wall.

There was a clock on top of Cecily's china closet. Angel had been watching it, counting down the moments until they would have to leave to catch the sleigh back to Yule Tide. But he also knew that they couldn't leave yet. Cecil's story had been eloquent but, Angel knew, it was only hearsay. He needed more.

"Mrs. Zagnutt," he asked, "can you take us to that grave?"

She shuddered. "I told myself that I'd never visit that place again. But that don't make no never mind. I see it every night. Every night when I crawl into my cold, empty bed. Every time I close my eyes." She paused, then nodded. "Yes, I'll take you."

Heading to the door, Billy patted at the down parka he still wore over his uniform. Cecily wrapped herself up in her bulky cloak then proceeded back into her bedroom and emerged with what appeared to be a blanket made from animal skin. Handing it to Angel, she said, "I'd lend you Gimbel's old parka. Still have it. It's a good un. Made from reindeer. Skin on the outside, fur on the in. Warm as the memory of a baby being born. But with your size? You'd never get in it. Here. Wrap yourself up in this. It's pretty frosty outside the walls."

"Pretty frosty inside the walls, too," Angel said.

Cecily managed a smile. "You ain't seen nothin' yet."

The streets outside were silent as they made their way down the dimly lit sidewalk and into the pitch black that lay beyond. When they had arrived at the Pole, the sky above had been stippled with stars. But clouds had since gathered shrouding even their glow. It was December at the Pole, only days away from the winter solstice, the season where the sun slumbers long behind the horizon awaiting the call of spring.

Angel reached into a pocket and pulled out his flashlight. Cecily noticed and shook her head. "Better we don't draw no attention to ourselves," she said. "Don't worry. I know the way. Been in the dark so long now I'm practically an owl."

It took about fifteen minutes for them to reach the outer walls of the campus. They followed tire tracks that could only just be made out in the gloaming. Once, along the way, the distant whir of an engine and the scrunching of tires reached them. Angel turned in time to see a far-off flash of headlights on the horizon. But they quickly blinked into nothingness.

At last, a halo of light appeared ahead and soon they reached a light pole that appeared like an apparition before them, illuminating a section of wall and a wide, rollup door. "This is where they get the wagons through to that…that place," Cecily said.

"Is there an alarm?" Billy asked.

Cecily nodded. "Damn right there is. Last time somebody tried to scoot through there you'd a thought there was a dang-blamed air raid goin' on. The freakin' sirens was that loud."

"So, how are we going to—" Billy began.

"Now don't get your knickers in a twist, Billy boy," Cecily interrupted. "I'll show you."

Angel and Billy followed as Cecily made her way along the wall, leading them once again across a barren, dark terrain.

But before long Angel could make out the outline of an expanse of bushes, probably junipers, several feet tall, wide and thick, growing next to the wall.

"This way," Cecily said as she ducked and disappeared into the bushes, Billy on her heels.

It was tough going, especially for Angel. Taller and broader than his companions, making his way through the scratchy bushes was a challenge. More than once the reindeer hide that he had draped across his shoulders snagged on the needles that sprouted like porcupine quills from the branches. But after passing through several feet of dense foliage, Angel spotted a hatch-like door, low to the ground, maybe four-foot by four-foot square. There was a simple, sliding bolt that fastened it secure. Cecily threw the bolt, the door swung open, there was a whoosh, and she ducked out beyond the wall.

Billy darted after her. Angel got on all fours and crawled through. Cecily closed the door behind them, securing it shut with a rock that had evidently been left there just for that purpose. Then she turned to continue their journey, Billy and Angel trailing her "It won't be long now," Angel heard an unseen Cecily say.

A shrieking wind created whirlwinds of the fine snow that now completely masked the vehicle tracks they had been following. The cold felt like an icy flame on Angel's cheeks and ears. He pulled the blanket more tightly around him, tucked his head down, and forged onward, led only by the sound of Cecily's footsteps crunching on the permafrost.

They walked maybe another ten minutes before Cecily reached back a hand to halt Billy. "We're here," she said.

It was difficult to make out anything in the murk, but the great expanse that spread into the distance before them appeared even blacker than the darkness that surrounded them—as though even the possibility of light had been sucked from the place.

Billy reached into his bag and pulled out his camcorder. He switched it on, held it up to his shoulder, and peered at the view screen that shown only minutely brighter than the inkiness before them.

Then Angel switched on his flashlight.

The beam revealed an open pit of some one hundred meters. The light first caught bright swathes of clothing rising through the snow. Then arms and legs akimbo, a great mass of twisted macabre statuettes. Hundreds of elves dumped like so much garbage into a frozen hellscape. Angel gazed at their faces. Preserved by the frigid temperatures, the faces were both young and old, eyes tightly shut, but some with mouths open in perpetual horror—teeth, some glinting bright and white in the beam from Angel's flashlight, others yellowed like dried corn. Angel sensed movement and swung the light to reveal a pair of arctic foxes several yards distant, moving stealthily among the frozen corpses, driving their snouts into the pile in search of fresh meat.

Billy, his camera making a slow sweep of the scene, swallowed loudly. Cecily drew a deep breath and sighed. "There's what's waitin' for us elves, boys," Cecily said. "That's where my Gimbel now rests."

"He deserved better," Angel said.

"They all did," Cecily replied.

After several minutes, Billy clicked off his camera, placed it back in his bag, and wordlessly, the trio turned to head back to the North Pole campus. To Santa's once magic village.

Chapter Twenty-Four

Cecily wasn't kidding about being part owl. Angel could scarcely believe her ability to directly lead them back through the darkness to the small door that allowed their entry inside the North Pole complex. She pushed away the rock that held the door in place, then ushered him and Billy inside. As Angel began to make his slow way through a juniper thicket, he heard Cecily slide the bolt which secured the door behind them. Once in the open, he looked to the sky. Clouds still predominated, but more dim points of stars glinted than before, as though a veil was slowly lifting. Although it was much colder inside the walls than Angel remembered from Kringle's day, at least it was warmer than the bone-numbing cold he had just escaped. He was grateful for the contrast.

When they were once again together, Billy stomped and flapped his arms several times to will warmth back into his extremities. Cecily watched quietly for some seconds before saying, "Let's get you boys on your way."

Billy quieted, then reached out a gloved hand and rested it briefly on her shoulder. "We can't thank you enough for all of your help, Ducks. We never could have done this without you."

"I just hope it's enough," she said. "Lord knows somethin's got to give."

Angel opened his mouth to respond, but a blinding light abruptly snapped on, pinning him where he stood. An amplified voice harshly blared, "Halt! Do not move!"

Angel's first thought was of preserving the video they'd recorded. "Run, Billy," he said softly, then began to wave his arms frantically over his head. The animal hide he'd used for warmth fell into a heap at his feet. Squinting against the light, Angel made out a jeep-like vehicle some thirty feet distant, its headlights directed toward him. "Thank goodness, you've found me!" Angel shouted. "I've been lost for hours."

Two silhouettes emerged from both sides of the jeep and stepped into the light—one with a hand on his hip, the other cradling what appeared to be a long gun.

Angel glanced around him. Both Cecily and Billy were gone.

"Do not move!" the voice repeated. "Put your hands on your head!"

Angel smiled. "Well, which is it? Do I put my hands on my head, or do I stop moving?"

"Put your hands on your head, smartass. Then don't move."

"That does make better sense."

Angel put his hands on his head and watched the twin figures approach. Both human, both male, they wore Company-issued, military-style uniforms— emerald-green jackets, red pants, black combat boots, and green Kevlar helmets—like the guards at the Gingerbread Mansion. One carried an M4 carbine. The other still had his sidearm holstered.

"There were others with you," the man with the rifle said, swinging his weapon before him. "Where did they go?"

"Others?" Angel asked. He shook his head. "No. Just me. And I can't tell you how happy I am that you came along. I was out for an evening stroll and must have wandered off too far. I had no idea how I was going to get back. I could have been lost out here for days. I was beginning to panic. You saved my life."

"I swear I saw some others with you. Looked like elves."

Angel answered with an expression of measured incredulity. "Now what would I be doing out here with elves?"

The second guard pulled his sidearm from its holster. "That's just what we'd like to know."

Angel shrugged. "Well, like I said, I've been out here for hours, and *I* haven't seen anyone." He paused. "By the way, can I put my arms down now?"

The second guard was a short man with a pug-like nose and blond hair that spilled voluminously from under his helmet. He stepped forward and pressed the barrel of his handgun none too gently just below Angel's sternum. "You do and I swear I'll put one through your pancreas."

Angel grinned. "Can't have that, can we?"

Several steps distant, the guard with the rifle shouted, "Quit gabbing with the prisoner and help me look for his accomplices. They can't have gotten far."

The blond guard sneered. "Just keep your hands on your head and don't move or it won't just be your pancreas. It'll be your spleen too."

Angel chuckled. "That's remarkably specific," he said. "Are you studying for your medical boards or something?"

The guard walked away without reply. Angel stayed in place as both guards switched on flashlights and began to search the immediate area for Cecily and Billy. After a couple of minutes, they returned to him. "You better tell us who you were out here with and what you were doing," Blondie warned.

"But I have told you already," Angel said pleasantly. "I was alone out for an evening's constitutional and became unfortunately disoriented."

"Let me see your ID."

"I'm afraid I left it back at my quarters. If you take me back there, I can get it for you."

"What's your name?"

"Angel. Harold Angel. What's yours?"

"None of your damned business," the blond guard snapped. "We're asking the questions."

"And doing a remarkable job of it, if I do say so," Angel replied. "If there's a survey of some kind at the end of this, I'd be happy to fill it out and give you both high marks."

"He's just wasting our time," Rifleman said. "I say we call for backup and do a thorough search of the area. I know I saw a couple of elves with this joker, and you know what the watch command has been telling us about rogue elves looking to harass operations. Could be this guy is in with...you know, a radical element."

"Sounds good. Let's cuff him and throw him in the back of the vehicle while we wait for another unit to arrive on scene."

Blondie unclipped a pair of handcuffs from his belt and approached Angel. "Hands behind your back, joker."

Angel lowered his hands and moved them around behind his back. But just as the guard was about to snap the cuffs on him, the headlights from their vehicle suddenly blinked off, enveloping them in darkness.

"What the…?" Rifleman exclaimed. He didn't have time to finish his question before multiple footsteps sounded around them and at least a dozen shadowy figures closed in. Short, shadowy figures.

When the headlights switched back on a moment later, the guards had been bound with cords and their weapons taken from them.

"Who are you…?" the blond guard began, but he was pulled to the ground and a rag stuffed into his mouth. The first guard, sensibly, kept silent.

An elf stepped forward. Middle-aged, for an elf, he was dressed simply in a pair of overalls, a corduroy jacket, and a fur-lined hat with long ear flaps. He carried a wooden staff, gripped with both hands. His eyes narrow and his mouth a grim line, the elf gave the staff a quick spin the way a trained martial artist might. Angel noted that the other elves were similarly armed. No firearms Just staffs, rakes, and other farm implements. They parted as the elf that Angel now took to be their leader approached him.

"Are you here to rescue me or to apprehend me?" Angel asked.

The elf's mouth widened into a smile. "To rescue you, of course," he said. "We're the Elfin Defense League. We'd been trackin' these two yahoos since they left the base. The Company likes to send out patrols. Not sure why. We generally let them go unmolested. But tonight? Well, tonight we thought we'd intervene."

"I'm grateful," Angel said.

"I didn't do it for you," the elf replied. "I did it for her."

The elf pointed to another figure slowly walking toward them. He then raised a hand and whoever was approaching halted. The elf then led Angel forward out of earshot of the immobilized guards.

"Hey, Angelpuss," Cecily Zagnutt greeted him as they reached her. "I see you've met me boy, Fizzwizz." Cecily beamed proudly. "Fizzwizz Zagnutt, meet Harold Angel.

Fizzwizz offered a hand. When Angel took it, Fizzwizz stared at him intently as though taking his full measure. After a moment, the elf released Angel's hand and nodded. "Mom says you might prove useful. We'll see. I'll have to reserve judgment on that. In the meantime, let's see about gettin' you on that sleigh home."

Billy appeared at Angel's side, clutching onto the bag with his camcorder the way a nervous toddler holds his teddy bear. He took a wary step forward as Fizzwizz turned to lead them back toward the village.

But Angel hesitated. "We've lost quite a bit of time," he said. "If we walk, I don't think we'll make the sleigh." He pointed toward the guards' vehicle. "Do you suppose we could borrow that?"

Fizzwizz paused, nodded, then reached up and squeezed Angel's arm. "Might be fun at that. I'll drive. You, your friend here, and Mom can all ride along. We won't be able to risk the lights, but I think we can get you back to the warehouse. After all, we have Mom with us. She's practically nocturnal. A night hunter."

"So we have seen," Angel said.

They returned to the guards and Fizzwizz pulled a handkerchief out of the pocket of his jacket, and unceremoniously shoved it into the mouth of the now-disarmed Rifleman. He made a few muffled attempts at crying out, but soon fell silent, plopping down on the ground next to his partner.

Angel picked up the animal hide that he had dropped and wrapped it around his shoulders before opening the front passenger side door. With a sweeping motion, he ushered Cecily in beside her son before joining Billy in the back seat. Fizzwizz rolled down his window and waved at his troops. "Go back to the base, me hearties. I'll be along as soon as I see these two off."

The elves let out a quiet, though heart-felt cheer as Fizzwizz turned away. He strained to reach the gas pedal and had to scoot to the very edge of the driver's seat to get his foot on it. When he finally made contact, his eyes were nearly parallel with the dashboard. Still, the jeep surged forward, gathering speed as it went, Fizzwizz directing it where his mom told him.

Taking a rather circuitous route to avoid the possibility of encountering other roving guards, they reached the warehouse without incident. Fizzwizz pulled up maybe twenty-five yards from rear of the building. Far enough to be outside the halo of light that surrounded it. He killed the engine and they listened.

Muted voices sounded from within the warehouse and Angel thought he could make out the scraping of hooves on the floorboards inside. And there was a distinct jingling of bells. He looked at his watch. The good news was that they still had ten minutes before the sleigh was scheduled to take off.

"How ya plannin' to get yerselves on that sleigh?" Fizzwizz asked.

"I was wondering that too, Boss," Billy said.

Angel sighed. "Well, I know there's a back door on the left side of the building. Doc Praetorius told me that. He said it would be unlocked until after the sleigh takes off. So, we should be able to get inside. Doc explained that once the crew unloads the cargo, they generally leave. A little later, a team of stable elves arrives with the reindeer that will be pulling the sleigh. I had hoped to get here earlier. Earlier enough to observe the unloading crew leave and to enter the warehouse before the stable elves arrive with the reindeer team."

Angel glanced at his watch again. "Sounds to me like the reindeer are already inside and harnessed. That means that even if the crew is gone and the driver has yet to arrive, when we enter, we'll be spotted by the stable elves. That will pose a problem. They would likely sound the alarm."

"Sounds bad, Boss," Billy said.

"You're right, Mr. Angel," Fizzwizz said. "Stable elves are extremely devoted to their reindeer. It's a bond that goes back centuries. If they view ya as a threat, they wouldn't just sound the alarm. They'd take you out. They're known to be…I guess you'd say they're fiercely protective."

"I'd rather that didn't happen," Angel said.

Fizzwizz smiled crookedly. "Me neither. But if it's just the elves in there. I mean, if the human crew's gone home and the human driver ain't here yet, I think we can get the elves to let you get on board. 'Course we'll need to let 'em know what yer up to and why ya need to hitch this ride. And we ain't got much time. Some of 'em probably know me. I'll go in with ya and we'll see what we can do." Fizzwizz shrugged. "I mean, what's the worst thing that can happen?"

"Umm," Billy said, stretching it out like taffy. "You just said they might kill us."

Angel ignored him. "Sounds like a plan, Mr.

Zagnutt," he said, clapping the elf on the shoulder.

"Boss…" Billy began.

Angel turned to his friend with a reassuring smile. "Oh, it'll be fine. We're going to make it. Trust me."

"There you go with that 'trust me' stuff again, Boss. You know what that does to my nerves."

"You just get on in there, Billy boy," Cecily said. "You're in good hands. Fizzy here's got friends everywhere. Them elves in there won't rat you out if he's with ya. Trust me."

"Now you're doing it," Billy said, his voice trembling.

Cecily laughed. "Stop frettin' now. You can do this."

She reached across the seat to give her son a hug before Angel, Billy and Fizzwizz quietly exited the vehicle. They slowly approached the rear door of the warehouse, taking even more deliberate steps as they entered into the light that cradled the structure. They were nearly to the door when they heard a metallic screeching coming from the front of the building. Angel pivoted, broke into a sprint, and headed around to the front door. Billy and Fizzwizz hurried after him.

As he ran, Angel distinctly heard the pounding of hooves, the rattle of the reins, and the tinkling of the bells. He reached the corner of the building in time to see the sleigh emerge from the warehouse. There was a whoosh as the containment system surrounding the campus was deactivated and the sleigh took a lazy turn to the left, straightened to exit through the now open gate, and lifted majestically into the sky.

The gate closed behind it and another whoosh signaled the containment system coming back on.

Billy and Fizzwizz joined Angel and, together, they watched as the lights on the rear of the sleigh raced out among the stars and finally disappeared into the distance.

Angel felt a hollow open within him, disappointment filling it like water spiraling into a whirlpool, threatening to drag him down with it. He'd had such hope. Now he just wanted a drink. More than one.

"What now?" Bill asked.

"I really don't know," Angel said. "I really don't know."

Chapter Twenty-Five

"I think I have an idea," Fizzwizz said. "It'll be dangerous, but it just might work."

Dejected over having missed the sleigh, the trio had returned to the stolen vehicle and rejoined Cecily. "I don't know how much more danger I can take," Billy said.

Angel lifted his head. "Let's hear your idea."

Fizzwizz stroked his chin with the tips of his fingers. "Might be better if I showed ya," he told them. "Hop back in. We'll drop Mom near the village, and I'll take ya to the Defense League's base of operations." He paused. "Okay. It's less a base than a shack. Still—"

"Ain't nobody gonna drop Mom off nowhere!" Cecily fumed. "I'm damned sure gonna see this through. I ain't come this far for you to—"

"Now, Ma," Fizzwizz replied, "it's late and you know how ya get if you short yerself on sleep."

Cecily took a deep breath and let it percolate within her like a boiler building steam. "Fizzwizz Pettifogger Zagnutt! What do ya take me fer? You think I'm some gol dern shrinkin' violet? Why I'll have ya know that I got more moxie in my little pinkie than you and that whole bunch of stick-carryin', do-goodin' fantasists ya run with." She paused. "The very idea! I'll go home when this thing's settled and not before. You hear me, boy?"

"Ah, Ma. It ain't a question of moxie. It's—"

Angel glanced back toward the warehouse. "Maybe we could have this conversation somewhere else," he suggested. "There might still be guards around."

Fizzwizz whipped his head around to scan the nearby building. "Gotcha," he whispered. "Y'all hop on in this here vehicle and we'll be on our way."

Cecily glared at her son.

"We'll *all* be on our way," Fizzwizz clarified. "You too, Ma. Wouldn't want to be deprived of all yer moxie, now, would we?"

They drove in silence through the dark for about fifteen minutes. Angel had nearly forgotten how large the North Pole complex was. Back in Kringle's day, although most elves lived in the village, some chose a more rural existence and were accommodated with houses and even barns on small tracks of land distant from the village and the workshop, yet still within the confines of the climate-controlled campus. As they drove, Angel could make out several of these parcels in the dim light. It appeared, however, that they had been abandoned. Some had been flattened, their foundations now empty bunkers, the structures gone, likely scavenged for firewood. A few still stood, roofs partially caved in, siding gone, skeletal frames creaking ominously.

At last, they reached their destination. Fizzwizz had called it a shack, but it was a fairly large one. Unlike the structures they'd had passed getting there, this appeared to be in reasonable repair. The building was tall with a gambrel roof, maybe fifteen hundred square feet, faded red siding, and a large double door trimmed in white. At least a dozen elves were gathered in front of those doors.

Fizzwizz Zagnutt's "hearties."

Fizzwizz brought the jeep to a stop and scurried around to open the passenger door for his mom. When Angel and Billy emerged from the vehicle, one of the elves, older than Fizzwizz, wearing a hooded woolen jacket—white, gray, and blue in a Norwegian design—stepped forward. Pointing, he said, "I figured they'd be on their way by now."

Fizzwizz shook his head. "Didn't make the sleigh. Gonna have to find another way to get 'em home."

"But why bring 'em here? If them Company goons are looking for 'em, they might track 'em here. Bit of a risk if you ask me."

"They won't be here long," Fizzwizz assured him.

The elf squinted but made no further reply.

"Come on inside," Fizzwizz said, motioning to Angel and Billy. "I've got somethin' to show you."

Fizzwizz led Angel, Billy, and Cecily to the door, slid back the bolt, and creaked it open just wide enough for them to slip through. Inside it was dark and damp, the sweet smell of hay mingling with the earthier scent of mildew. At first, it was utterly silent, then from the opposite side of the space came a distinct clicking sound. The clicking stopped, but after a moment came a sonorous, breathy bark.

Startled, Billy jumped, nearly dropping the bag that held his camcorder. "What was that?" he asked, the tremor in his voice threatening to morph into all out yodel.

"That," Fizzwizz said, "is what I have to show you."

Near the entrance to the building was a bench and on the bench a kerosene lantern and a box of matches. Fizzwizz picked up both and, striking the match on the rear of his trousers, touched the flame to the wick. Soft, yellow light filled the room.

"That there is Herschel," he said.

From out of the shadows stepped a reindeer. He had a prodigious rack, the lower part extending over his face, the upper part curving back over his shoulders before bowing aggressively forward—like a wave curling over itself as it breaks for the shore. He was an older animal, with a shaggy coat, a sagging belly, legs that appeared shorter than they should, and a hump between his shoulders. But his eyes were clear, black, and proud.

He let out another imposing chuff, then lumbered over to Fizzwizz.

"You sure about this, Fizzy?" Cecily asked.

"I'm sure, Ma."

When the reindeer reached him. Fizzwizz slipped his hand into a pocket and produced a small, green apple. The reindeer bowed his head. Fizzwizz opened his palm and with a loud smack, the apple was gone.

"You keep a reindeer?" Angel asked.

Fizzwizz nodded.

Angel raised an eyebrow. "He's…uh…He's… I guess you might call him mature."

"He's a ripe oldie, Mr. Angel. That's fer sure. Old enough that the Company retired him. That's what they call it. Retired. What it means is they was gonna put him down. The elf that raised him's a friend a mine. Didn't want to see old Herschel here go like that. Didn't want to see Herschel hacked up into steaks or ground into sausages neither."

Billy gasped. "He'd have been eaten?"

"Meat's scarce around here, Mr. Goodman," Fizzwizz explained. "Anyway, the Defense League's got this here shed and...Well, I guess I'm an old softie. I've been keepin' him here. Tryin' to figure out what the holy heck to do with him if ya want to know the truth. When I seen that sleigh take off and you two not on it, I got me an idea. Don't know's it's a good one, but I thought I'd run it by ya."

"And your idea is?" Angel asked.

"Herschel here is old, that's fer sure. But he was a good flyer in his day. One of the best. Even pulled lead for Santa hisself more than once. 'Course, that was a few years back. Still..."

"You expect us to ride him out of here?" Angel asked.

Fizzwizz laughed. "No. No. Nothin' like that. We got us a sleigh. Lookee over here."

He led them to a corner where something bulky was covered by a tarp sewed together from gunny sacks. Fizzwizz drew back the tarp to reveal a box-like contraption. Unlike Santa's elegant version or the workhorse cargo sleigh that Angel and Billy had arrived on, this was a simple design, a rectangular box about six feet long made of what looked like pine boards joined to one another with dovetails and reinforced with angle irons. There were no seats inside, but handrails were bolted on both sides, presumably to help keep the occupants from spilling out during flight.

"Looks like a coffin with runners," Billy observed.

"It does at that," Angel agreed.

Fizzwizz nodded. "I know it looks a fright, but it should hold together right enough. One of me boys, Hymie Upatree, made it. Hymie used to be head carpenter back in Kringle's day. Specialized in bird houses. Anyway, I was thinkin' that we could harness old Herschel up to this here sleigh. He's been pinin' away stuck in here. He's used to the sky. It'd give him one last chance to do what he's always done. Fly."

"One last chance?" Billy asked.

"Poor choice of words, maybe," Fizzwizz allowed.

Angel bent over to examine the sleigh in the lantern light. First, he gave it a good knock, then grasped a corner with both hands and applied pressure. It didn't give or let out so much as a squeak.

"If we do this," Angel said, "we're going to have to get outside the walls. We can't get aloft from here. We're inside the containment system. I don't see any way we could disrupt it. Even briefly. No. We're going to have to take this operation outside."

Fizzwizz nodded. "Well, you three have been outside there already this evenin'. No reason ya can't do it again."

Billy shook his head vigorously. "No way we're going to get this reindeer and that so-called sleigh through that tiny door in back of them junipers like we done before."

"And there are too many guards at the front gate for us to go out there," Angel added. "Looks like we'll have to use the larger back exit that Cecily showed us earlier."

Billy's mouth dropped open. "But she said that door has an alarm."

"It sure does," Cecily confirmed. "Loud enough to rattle the fillings plumb out yer molars."

"Won't that alert the authorities?" Billy asked.

"They'll come a runnin' sure as night follows day," Cecily told him.

"Then we can't possibly—" Billy began.

"I wonder how long it would take for a patrol to

reach the door once the alarm sounds," Angel interrupted.

"Depends on how far out they patrolin'," Fizzwizz told him. "Somewhere between ten minutes and right away."

"Boss," Billy beseeched, "we can't take that chance. If we get caught, we lose the video. We lose the evidence we came for. Now, I say we hunker down and wait for the next cargo sleigh. We can time it better then. It's only two weeks. We can hide out here that long."

"But we'd miss Christmas," Angel said.

"We can celebrate after we get back. Heck, Orthodox Christmas ain't until January 7th. We'd be back by then." Billy smiled. "I wouldn't want to miss out on any present you might have squirreled away for me."

"It's not our missing Christmas together that I'm worried about," Angel said. "Presenting our evidence before the 25th gives us leverage. Right now, most of the world's thoughts are focused on the upcoming holiday. Revealing to the public just how the Company is treating elves at the Pole would turn that happy expectation to horror. Scratch and the Company can't have that. It would shake the very foundation of their operation. If we fail to confront them with what we have before Christmas, we lose that leverage. People have remarkably short attention spans. If we're too late, people will have moved on. Their thoughts turned to the next thing. The next distraction. We need to do everything we can to get back as soon as possible. Before Christmas."

"But the guards! The patrol!" Billy exclaimed. "If they hear that alarm. If they catch us."

"Got me an idea about that too," Fizzwizz said. "Us

elves in the Defense League have been studyin' on how best to shake things up around here. You know. Put the Company on notice. No sense in raisin' troops and havin' 'em do nothin'. Now if we was to be at that door when them Company goons come roarin' up, and us waitin' in the dark, well, I reckon we might be able to dissuade them from followin' y'all long enough to for you to get airborne."

"They have firearms," Angel reminded him.

A crooked smile broke across Fizzwizz's face. "They do. But we've bested 'em before. We can do it again." He turned to his mom. "Besides, we have somethin' they don't got. Moxie. We's just loaded with moxie."

Cecily beamed, pride nearly masking the apprehension in her eyes. "That settles it," she said. "Fizzy, you round up them troops of yers and we'll set about gettin' that reindeer hitched up. Gonna be a helluva thing seein' you boys in the air. I wouldn't miss it fer nothin'."

Billy sighed. "I'd miss it for just about anything."

Chapter Twenty-Six

Fizzwizz and a few of his men hoisted the sleigh to the top of the purloined jeep and strapped it tight. He then loaded Billy and a few of his men inside. Herschel was too big for them to transport, so Angel elected to walk alongside the elderly reindeer with Cecily in the lead. As they made their way through the dark, Herschel's joints clicked noticeably. Angel had heard this referred to as "a voice from the bones," common to reindeer which evolved to help keep the members of a herd in contact with one another during snowstorms. In this case, the clicking of the solitary reindeer—caused by the friction of a tendon slipping over a bone in the back feet—spoke eloquently of Herschel's exile from his kind. There was no herd for him to stay in contact with.

It was a long, slow, dark walk. There were times that Herschel's legs did not appear to adequately support his weight and he'd stumble. Angel began to doubt the wisdom of their decision to try to fly back to Yule Tide. Especially as Herschel's breathing seemed to become more and more labored as they went.

A couple of times Cecily halted them, raising a palm, and listening intently. One of those times Angel heard the sound of a distant engine. The other time he heard nothing.

When they finally reached the door at the rear of the North Pole campus, they found several elves gathered just outside the halo cast by the light pole that towered over the fence. Clustered around the jeep, most were armed with sticks or farm implements. Fizzwizz had exchanged his staff for a shepherd's sling that he'd draped over one shoulder, a cloth bag bulging with what Angel assumed were stones over the other. Fizzwizz smiled as Angel and Herschel approached.

"Made it this far, I see," he said.

Angel merely nodded.

Billy joined them and Fizzwizz ordered his troops to haul the sleigh from the top of the jeep and bring it forward.

"You ready for this, Mr. Angel?" he asked.

"I am." He paused. "The Company will come after us. This could get dangerous. Are you ready for that, Mr. Zagnutt?"

"Ready as a fox for the hunt," Fizzwizz declared.

Angel smiled. "Just look out the hounds don't catch you."

"Never you mind about that," Fizzwizz said. Casting his gaze toward his diminutive militia he added, "Them hounds is all bark. We got us some bite."

Angel chuckled.

The rigging had already been secured to the sleigh and two elves approached Herschel with the harness they'd use to tether him to it. Herschel lowered his head willingly when they reached him, allowing them to secure it around his neck—just behind his ears—as well as encircling his muzzle. He gave his head a grateful nod as they led him to the sleigh and fastened him to the rigging. Then one of the elves clipped a short string of sleigh bells to the underside of Herschel's harness. As he did, the bells jingled merrily. Herschel opened his mouth wide at the sound, then shook his head repeatedly, filling the air with chimes, and showing his teeth in a jubilant smile. He gave a hearty snort and pressed his snout warmly against the elf who had brought him the bells. The elf smiled as well, reaching high to rub the reindeer behind an ear. Herschel lifted his head, snorted again, and cast his eyes skyward.

"He looks ready," Angel said.

"He looks ancient," Billy countered.

"He'll be fine," Angel assured him. "Don't worry."

Billy glared but did not reply.

"Okay, this is it," Fizzwizz said. "You two hop in the sleigh and we'll get ya through that door. It's locked but that'll be no trouble. We're good with locks. The trouble will come when the gol dern alarm goes off."

Angel clapped Fizzwizz on the shoulder but said nothing. Then he and Billy climbed into the sleigh. It was a tight fit. Angel sat in front, his knees against his chest to allow room for Billy to sit behind him.

Billy glanced over to Cecily who stood nearby, her mouth set in a grim line, her eyes shining with tears.

"Goodbye, Ducks," Billy said. "It was good to see you again."

Cecily stood still for a moment before waving a dismissive hand. "Off with ya, ya old scallywag," she said, but followed up with a distinct sob.

Angel took hold of the reins and Billy clutched the handrails as Herschel moved forward and the traces tightened.

"Get 'er open!" Fizzwizz ordered and an elf scurried toward the gate with a long, needle-like implement which she inserted into the lock. After a moment there was a click. The elf glanced at Fizzwizz who nodded back at her. The elf reached down, grasped the bottom of the door, and rolled it up and open.

Immediately, the air was rent by an earsplitting siren. It was so loud that many of the elves clapped hands over their ears and stumbled backward. One toppled over.

Seeing the open door, Herschel lurched forward, driving Angel and Billy to the rear as the sleigh doddered toward the exit. Angel scooted himself back into position and glanced behind them in time to see Fizzwizz take the cord ends of his sling in one hand and place a stone in the pouch. The elf then drew back and swung it over his head, as though throwing a baseball, before letting go of one of the cords. The stone flew from the pouch straight and true smashing into the fixture atop the light pole, plunging everything into darkness.

Herschel began to trot, and the sleigh built up speed. They were through the door and out into the cold and snow, the siren whooping behind them. The reindeer huffed loudly, breathing deep, then releasing it with a wheezy rattle. They were maybe fifty yards past beyond the perimeter when Angel heard it. A high-pitched buzzing sound above them. He raised his eyes and saw a glinting green light hovering there. A drone, he realized. There was more buzzing and more green lights in the sky gaining on them. Probably sending live video back to Company security, Angel thought.

Looking back toward the still open door, Angel caught glimpses of several more drones bobbing unsteadily over where the elfin militia had been positioned. There was a pinging sound and one of the drones fell abruptly to the ground. Fizzwizz and his sling, Angel speculated.

Then beams of light shone in the distance jouncing as they approached. Vehicles coming their way, Angel realized. They had to get in the air, or they would be caught.

As if reading Angel's thoughts, Herschel surged forward and his front legs both lifted from the ground. But his rear legs stayed stubbornly on terra firma. The reindeer lowered his large head, his antlers pointed forward, rending the air before them. He pushed into a sprint and all at once he was airborne.

The sleigh jerked into the sky behind him, both Angel and Billy holding on for dear life.

Once aloft, a trio of drones moved in on them, darting erratically. One got too close to Herschel who, with a shake of his head, clipped it hard with his antlers. The drone dropped out of sight, but Herschel had lost momentum, and the sleigh plunged several feet before the reindeer recovered and they resumed their ascent. Another drone buzzed the sleigh coming within reach of Billy who batted at it with a gloved hand. The drone wobbled and one of the propellers hit the side of the sleigh. There was a snapping sound and the drone plummeted into the darkness below them.

Herschel seemed invigorated by the icy wind that now whipped around them. As another drone gained on them from the rear, Herschel trumpeted what Angel interpreted as a laugh before he sped away, leaving the drone behind them. Before they reached maximum speed, Angel looked back and saw that the headlights of the Company vehicles had reached the back fence. He could only hope that Fizzwizz and his hearties had found safety. Soon the sleigh was well out of reach.

The trip home turned out to be largely uneventful.

They hit some turbulence as they dashed south over the polar ice cap, but conditions eventually smoothed. Angel scanned the surface for some landmark by with to measure their journey, but soon the dark ice was replaced with the even darker waters of the Arctic Ocean. Angel remembered when it took far longer to reach open water from the Pole. Climate change, he thought. Polar ice receding like the mist of a dimly remembered past.

Billy shivered beside him, tucking his head into his parka, and letting go an occasional whimper. But Herschel had found his stride. His breathing was steady. His head held high and proud.

Soon, Angel spotted land and some lights below. Probably Cambridge Bay, he told himself, a small hamlet on Canada's Victoria Island. Part of the Arctic Archipelago. Angel had flown over many times before losing his wings.

Somewhere over the Northwest Territories, Billy fell asleep, his arm wrapped around the bag that held his camcorder. Angel thought about the video they'd shot—their one chance at making the world see the truth about the Company. He also thought about the coming confrontation with Scratch and about how, when they opposed him, both Claus the Second and Luther Deo had simply disappeared.

Angel craned his neck to watch his friend sleep for a moment then turned around to watch the triumphant reindeer pull them steadily onward in what Angel reflected might be the last flight for them both.

Chapter Twenty-Seven

It wasn't Herschel's last flight.

The sleigh touched safely down in the parking lot of a shuttered big box store at the edge of Yule Tide. Angel and Billy crawled out and Angel unbuckled Herschel's harness. Placing a palm against the reindeer's muzzle Angel leaned in and said softly, "Thank you."

Herschel snorted, then turned his eyes skyward.

"We'll find you somewhere safe for the rest of the night," Angel assured the reindeer. "We'll find you some grass or leaves or something else to eat and tomorrow we'll start looking for a new home for you." Angel paused. "I'm afraid you can't go back to the Pole, old fellow. Even if the guards let you back in, you've been retired. It would be like…like…"

Herschel pawed at the ground, shook his head several times, and snorted again. Then he raised his head and licked the side of Angel's face with a large, wet, pebbly tongue. Angel smiled and patted the reindeer's muzzle once again. Then Herschel stepped back, swung around, and broke into a trot, racing for the distant fence at the other end of the parking lot. Before he reached it, Herschel was in the air. Moments later, he was gone.

"Brave animal," Billy observed. "He's facing an uncertain future."

Angel reached out and touched the bag that Billy was holding—the bag with the camcorder. "As are we all, my friend."

Ditching the sleigh in the shadows alongside the deserted building, Angel and Billy walked to a nearby gas station and called for an Uber. Before long they were back at Billy's room.

Dawn was breaking as Billy went to work plugging the camcorder into his computer and downloading the video. "I'll upload it to my cloud storage," he said. "But what do we do next, Boss?"

Sitting across from him on Billy's bed, Angel leaned back and closed his tired eyes. When he opened them, he stood and joined Billy at his worktable. Writing something on a notepad Angel said, "I know a guy who works for the local affiliate for one of the major networks. This is his email address. He was a client a couple of years back. Things turned out well for him. I think if we give him the video, he'd at least check it out. It's important that someone outside of this room has a copy. That way if I suddenly disappear after I visit Scratch someone would—"

"After you visit Scratch?" Billy exclaimed. "We got the goods. Why would you visit Scratch? Let the media handle it from here. Them newsies take one look at what we shot at that mass grave, hear what Cecily has to say about how the Company's been lying to them, they're gonna be madder than a wet hen. There ain't no need for you go poking that bear yourself."

Angel sighed. "This has been a long time coming, Billy. This thing between Scratch and me. That video of yours might be enough to bring the Company down a notch or two, but it's also possible that they will be able spin their way out of it. They have been quite successful with that up until now. No. No matter what happens, I will have my moment with Scratch.

Billy looked up at his friend and swallowed hard. "If you're going, Harry, I'm going too."

Angel gave him a weary smile. "No, Billy. I need you out here. In case something goes south. I need to know that someone is still out here trying to make things right." He paused. "Or else all those elves will have died in vain."

Billy shook his head. "I'm no hero, Harry."

"Sure, you are, Billy. You've proved it before, and you proved it again last night. And besides, there's no telling how this will end." Angel chuckled. "Who knows? I might actually be successful."

"Well, sure, Boss, but—"

Angel's cellphone rang. When he put it to his ear, a familiar voice said, "They're watching the front of the building. Do you think you can leave by the rear? Undetected?"

"Mr. Dickens. What a pleasant surprise. You're up early."

"Thanks to you, Mr. Angel, I've had no sleep at all," Fenster Dickens informed him. "I was up all night, monitoring reports from the Pole. It seems that someone managed to infiltrate the North Pole complex. No one is certain who it was or what they were doing there but there is video of an escape. It's too grainy to make out who they were, but a pair of suspects are visible taking off in a small, rustic-looking sleigh pulled by a reindeer reportedly old enough to have been reared by a teenaged Methuselah."

"Gee, I hope nothing important is missing."

"Come now, Mr. Angel. Let's stop playing. I need to talk to you. If you can leave undetected, you'll find me at The Blue Carbuncle. It's a pub on Nutcracker Street. I'm afraid you will have to hurry. I can only wait a short time. Say, fifteen minutes?"

"It's a bit early for pub crawling, isn't it, Mr. Dickens?"

"Tish tosh, old boy. The pub's not open at this hour. But I know the proprietor. If you can join me, I assure you that we will have the place to ourselves."

"And to what do I owe this invitation?"

Dickens' laugh was high-pitched, like that of a child. It contrasted starkly with the weight of his words. "Because you *owe* me, Mr. Angel. It was I that sent Morningstar to you. It was I who provided you the audio recording of Luther Deo's last moments. I have risked everything and now all I ask is a meeting. Is that so much?"

"No. I suppose not. I'll be there shortly."

"See that you are not followed."

It was Angel's turn to laugh. "Oh, I think I can manage that."

****

The Blue Carbuncle was in a section of town that some had begun referring to as Rivendell after the hidden valley in Tolkien's Middle-earth. About three blocks long and two blocks wide, the area supported several elf-owned businesses specializing in things like clothing, furniture, even tableware, all scaled appropriately for the city's elfin population. And the case in a popular neighborhood meat market was reliably filled with caribou roasts and large filets of salted fish—foods fondly remembered by those who'd emigrated from the Pole.

The façade of The Blue Carbuncle resembled a

traditional English pub—white-washed brick, windows trimmed in black, and hanging above the door a large wooden sign with a caricature of Sherlock Holmes, a deerstalker on his head, peering intently down his long nose through a magnifying glass at what Conan Doyle described as a "brilliantly scintillating" blue gemstone.

The door to the pub was locked but Angel tapped on its glass window and an elf—totally bald and wearing a white apron—opened the door for him, locking it immediately behind them.

The interior of the pub was dark, illuminated only by pendant lamps that hung from the ceiling and a few dim carriage lights fixed to the walls—walls covered in blue paper suffused with just a hint of green. Along one side of the room, the seating was comprised of booths with walnut tables and high-back seats of tufted brown leather. Above the booths were framed advertisements for English beers—Elgood's Black Dog, Fuller's London Porter, and something called Shepherd Neame's Bishops Finger among them. More tables filled the interior of the space—most round and low to the ground surrounded by elf-sized wooden chairs, but a number of human-sized chairs were also scattered about indicating that The Blue Carbuncle served a diverse clientele. Fenster Dickens—dressed as though he'd just emerged from Saville Row in a double-breasted light gray suit over a navy-blue dress shirt and a blue tie with a white slide stripe—sat at a table in front of a low bar fronted with diminutive bar stools. Dickens' hands were folded on top of the table. Seated in a taller chair, Gloria Deo towered over him.

She was wearing a cobalt-blue tea dress, short-sleeved with fabric-covered buttons that ran from her waist to a V-neckline. It was calf-length but rode up as she sat there, showcasing her long legs. Angel caught his breath at the sight of her.

When he reached the table, Dickens stood and extended a hand. "Thank you for agreeing to meet me," he said.

"My pleasure," Angel replied. He glanced at Mrs. Deo. "I expected to meet you alone. Although, naturally, finding Mrs. Deo here with you is also a pleasure."

"Will you have a seat, Mr. Angel?" Dickens asked, indicating a nearby chair.

Angel pulled the chair over and took a seat at Dickens' table. Leaning in, he asked the elf "How much does she know?"

"Oh, dear me, Mr. Angel," Dickens replied, "only what you may have told her."

Mrs. Deo reached up and brushed at a lock of hair that had fallen across her face. "Mr. Dickens told me that you had information about my missing Luther. He invited me here with the expectation that you would tell me what you know."

Angel arched an eyebrow at Dickens before turning to Mrs. Deo. "I'm afraid I have no definite information. But I am in possession of an audio recording of your husband's last meeting with the Claus and Mr. Scratch. It was delivered to me at great expense by an elf in employ of your friend Noel Baba."

"Great expense?" Mrs. Deo asked. "Whatever do you mean by—"

"This tape," Angel interrupted, "features a conversation between those three that ends abruptly and, may I say, suspiciously. It is as though your husband was there one moment and simply gone the next."

"You mean he left suddenly?" Mrs. Deo pressed.

"Yes, but I suspect by means other than the door."

Mrs. Deo shook her head and that lock of hair fell back across her face. "I'm afraid I don't understand."

Angel sighed. "I'm afraid I don't either. The tape is inconclusive. But we now know who were the last to speak with your husband. They know what happened to him. What we don't know is if they will be willing to tell us."

Dickens continued to sit silently beside them. It struck Angel that this was normal for Dickens—to be in the room but seemingly apart from what is happening there.

"Were you there, Mr. Dickens?" Angel asked. "Were you in the room for that last meeting between Mr. Deo, the Claus, and Scratch?"

"I was not."

"But you know what occurred."

Dickens nodded. "There is a malevolence at work, Mr. Angel. An evil so strong it creates its own gravity. It is tangible and it is anchored at least in part by Mr. Nicolas Scratch."

Angel remembered the wooziness he experienced in Scratch's office. "I've felt it."

"When you visited Scratch the other day?"

Angel nodded.

"The meeting was unscheduled," Dickens said, "but I make it a point to know with whom he is meeting. And why."

"And why do you think I met with him?"

A corner of Dicken's mouth curled. "You are looking to destroy him, of course. To find a chink in his armor. That is why I decided to help you."

"You had a recording device in Scratch's office. You are monitoring his conversations."

Dickens made a brief bow of his head. "Yes. Ever since the disappearance of Claus the Second." He paused. "I looked up to him, Mr. Angel. I believed in his potential to help safeguard Christmas and those who make it possible. They say that he died in a tragic accident. But no one saw this accident and no one I've talked to ever saw his body. It was as though he simply disappeared."

"Like Luther?" Gloria Deo asked.

Dickens nodded. "Like Luther."

"Are you with the National Association for Elfin Rights, Mr. Dickens?" Angel asked.

"NAER." Dickens chuckled. "I lobbied hard against that name. It's so. . .so obvious."

"Was Luther Deo also involved in the organization?"

Dickens wrinkled his brow. "Only indirectly. Mr. Deo came to suspect that he wasn't being told the whole truth about how retired elves were being cared for. He also came to suspect that I shared his suspicions and might be of some help. He was a man who believed deeply in Christmas and its traditions. He vowed that if elves at the Pole were being neglected, he would change that. But he needed more information. I cautioned him to be wary of directly confronting other high-ranking Company officials. Instead, I put him in touch with others active in NAER. I must say he was a very meticulous man. He gathered his information slowly. Painstakingly. He rarely spoke directly to NAER operatives but devised various codes, various signals that he used to communicate with them."

Angel nodded. "The eyebrow thing."

Dickens raised both of his eyebrows. "My compliments," he said. "You are, of course, referring to that interview Mr. Deo did with the media where he thoroughly discredited the reports of elfin mistreatment while simultaneously conveying to NAER operatives that he had important information to pass on. He did that by plucking out a code as he tugged at his eyebrow. Ingenious, really."

Angel hummed. "And yet I wonder how devoted he was to the NAER cause. As I recall there was a bonus. A rather large and suspiciously timed bonus of one hundred thousand dollars that the Company made to Deo. Was that in reward for the exemplary job he was doing as the Claus' assistant or for something else?"

Dickens sat back in his chair. "Deo was a good man. Good at his job. And certainly deserving of compensation. And while that particular renumeration may have been made in part to dissuade him from looking into matters at the Pole, it did so only momentarily. When I became aware of it, I went to him. I reminded him of what was at stake. I then made arrangements for him to travel to the Pole to see for himself the privations visited upon the residents there. To see the bodies." Dickens paused. "After that, there was no force that could stop him from confronting Scratch. If only he'd come to me first. Strategized with me as to the best way of going forward. But I'm afraid he became so dismayed by what he had discovered that he acted rashly. He went to Scratch alone and became lost to us."

Next to him, Angel heard Mrs. Deo let out a single sob, but so softly it was the coo of a distant mourning dove.

Angel paused. "You say you sent Gabriel Morningstar to me."

"I did. But somehow his mission was discovered. And he died because of it."

"Who is Gabriel Morningstar?" Mrs. Deo asked.

Angel turned to look into her green eyes. They shimmered with both barely checked tears and steely resolve—waring emotions wresting with one another beneath the surface calm.

"He is the elf I mentioned," Angel explained. "The one who worked at The Night Visitor."

Mrs. Deo took an audible breath. "Is Noel involved in all of this? Did he have anything to do with Luther's—"

"I really don't know, Mrs. Deo," Dickens said. "Mr. Baba is like the rest of us. He owes his position to Scratch. He is willing to do him favors. To overlook certain happenstances. Some of which are quite troubling. But I do not know if he was directly involved."

"Is Luther..." Mrs. Deo began, "is Luther dead?"

"I wish I could tell you, ma'am," Dickens said. "All I know is that until now an impenetrable evil has been at work. I maneuvered myself into my current position as the Claus' valet in order to work against that evil. I'm afraid that I have been less than successful. My hope is that Mr. Angel here will have more success."

"Just how do you propose I do that?" Angel asked.

Dickens smiled. "You traveled to the Pole. Did you get what you were looking for?"

"I believe so."

"And that was?"

"Testimonies. Photographic evidence of the

Company's criminal neglect of their former employees. Elfin bodies dumped in a pile like so much garbage. The footage is…quite compelling."

"Useful," Dickens said. "That should prove useful. Along with the audio tape of Scratch's last meeting with your husband, Mrs. Deo, it could be enough to…How shall I say it? Dislodge Mr. Scratch's control of the Company."

"The Claus appears on that audio tape as well," Angel pointed out. "You are his assistant. If he falls along with Scratch, you would be out of a job."

Dickens sighed. "Scratch arranged the election of our current Claus for a good reason. I'm afraid our current Santa lacks what you might call a penetrative mind. But he is of a good heart if not of a bold one. If this thing is properly managed, I think he can survive."

"Does he know what is going on at the Pole?"

"Define 'know'," Dickens replied. "Does he have reason to believe that the stories are true? Yes. Does he have personal knowledge that they are true? No, he does not. If we are successful and this thing blows up, his ignorance might be enough to save him."

Angel was silent for a moment. "I find you a most interesting elf, Mr. Dickens. You work in the highest reaches of the Company yet conspire with NAER to bring it down. You were loyal enough to appear to agree with the Claus that I end my investigation of elfin mistreatment at the Pole yet sent me the very thing that would prompt my doing exactly that. How do I know that our discussion here this morning is not another misdirection?"

"Frankly, Mr. Angel, you do not."

Angel nodded. "Can you tell me the real reason that

you invited Mrs. Deo to join us this morning? I don't believe it was to provide her closure. Not at this time. Not with so many things in motion. What role are you expecting her to play?"

"You misjudge me, Mr. Angel," Dickens said. "I do want her to know the truth. I want everyone to. Now I will admit that it occurred to me that her appearance before the media along with whatever evidence you can provide might prompt the fourth estate to rethink what has been their indifference to the myriad allegations against the Company. A grieving spouse seeking the truth about her missing husband will definitely play better than easily libeled elves making wild claims of malfeasance."

"So, you are using her?"

"My dear Mr. Angel, I am using you both."

Angel started to respond but Mrs. Deo spoke first. "If Mr. Scratch has cost me my husband, I am willing to do whatever it takes to bring about his downfall."

Angel reached out and took her hand. "But that could mean—"

She squeezed his hand. "Whatever it takes," she repeated.

Dickens rubbed his palms together and stood. "It's settled then. Our next step will be to orchestrate an appearance in the media. I have several contacts that I can reach out to. I will be in touch later today. We must strike right away. Before Christmas is behind us."

The elfin proprietor of The Blue Carbuncle approached Dickens and whispered something that Angel could not quite make out.

Dickens nodded. "It has been suggested that we make our egress through the rear of this establishment.

Follow me."

Angel frowned. He turned to look at Mrs. Deo. Her features were set, a flinty determination in her eyes. The proprietor led them behind the bar and through a small kitchen to a heavy metal door in the rear. When he opened it, Angel immediately spotted the blue van parked in the back alley.

Balthasar's right arm was still in a sling from his altercation with Angel, but he held a shiny blue gun in his left hand. Melchior, sporting a pulpy bulge on the left side of his head, stood beside him with knife drawn. Caspar stood next to the open van door, one hand squeezing the shoulder of a trembling Billy Goodman.

Balthasar smiled thinly. "Now that our company is all together," he said, "let us be off. Someone you all know is most anxious to chat with you."

Chapter Twenty-Eight

The door to Scratch's office at Company headquarters opened slowly. Angel had been surprised to find the entire thirty-fourth floor empty when Balthasar and his pair of ruffians pushed them from the elevator into the hallway. This close to Christmas, the space should have been bustling with employees tending to last minute details. But they were totally alone. No one to witness what might occur.

Angel entered the office first, followed by Gloria Deo, Billy, and Fenster Dickens, the three wise guys bringing up the rear. As before, the office was dimly lit, Scratch's goose necked lamp turned to illuminate the emptiness in front of his desk while he, seated behind it, remained in relative darkness. But enough light seeped in from the edges of the drawn curtains for Angel to make out both the black leather-bound tome that Scratch kept on his desk as well as two additional figures in the room. The Claus and Noel Baba stood against the wall, both motionless, as though at attention.

"Welcome back, dear boy," Scratch said. His voice, usually filled with melancholy, seemed somehow buoyant. "And such lovely company you bring with you. I don't believe I've had the pleasure of meeting your diminutive adjutant, Mr. Goodman. But, of course, it's a pleasure to see you again, Mrs. Deo." He paused. "And finally, our beloved Santa's major domo, Mr. Dickens.

Delightful. Had I been expecting you I'd have had canapés brought in."

Angel smirked. "You had us kidnapped. It's difficult to believe that you weren't expecting us."

Scratch leaned forward and appeared to wave a dismissive hand. But dark as it was, he could have been brushing away spiders. "I only meant that there was little time to prepare for your arrival."

"And yet," Angel pressed, "you had time to summon both Santa and Mr. Baba. Might I ask to what they owe the invitation?"

"I thought it best," Scratch said, "to bring everyone associated with the Luther Deo situation together. The better to see where each of us stands."

"I agree. I would like to know where Santa and Mr. Baba stand," Angel said. "As for me, I stand for justice."

Scratch laughed—a high, grinding sort of laugh like a rasp working on metal. "Justice? Justice, dear boy, is like a lost feather drifting on a breeze. Impossible to predict where it might light or for how long. In any case, I do apologize for the suddenness with which I summoned you all here. I only learned within the last hour of the events that occurred yesterday evening at what I'd heretofore believed was our secure North Pole facility. I don't mean to make rash accusations, but I'm wondering if our Mr. Dickens delayed those reports from reaching me. It turns out that he has been a bit of a rascal for some time. But never mind. The truth has a way of revealing itself."

"Again, I agree," Angel said. "This has, after all, been about uncovering the truth. The truth about Luther Deo's disappearance. The truth about conditions at the Pole. The truth about what you and your organization have done to Christmas."

"I must give you credit, Angel. Here you are cornered in my office—my sanctum sanctorum—with, I assure you, no means of escape and you don't try to bargain. You remain steadfast to your goal of discrediting us. I must commend you. You are a true believer."

Angel bowed slightly.

Scratch smiled. "You are, no doubt familiar with the saying 'The mind is its own place and, in itself can make a heaven of hell or a hell of heaven.'"

"Milton," Angel observed.

"Satan," Scratch corrected. "And knowing both of you, I'd say you have something in common. You both have fixed and rather fanatical points of view. Diametrically opposed, it's true, but I find that zealotry of any stripe inevitably leads to destruction. True belief clouds our minds and cloaks the truth. Goals are laudable, but our pursuit of them must be tempered with practicality. With self-preservation. For if in pursuing your goal, you lean too heavily toward self-sacrifice, you risk becoming diminished. And then what good are you to others? You've become a drain instead of a boon."

Scratch reached out and turned the beam of his desk lamp to shine more entirely on Angel and his companions. "You also become a risk to those foolish enough to believe in you."

Angel glanced at the others. Billy was breathing heavily—his shoulders hunched, his head down. Fenster Dickens appeared completely self-composed. He might have been waiting for a bus. But Gloria Deo stood tall, defiant, her eyes glistening with hate and a rapier-sharp desire for revenge.

"You think you've won, Mr. Scratch," Angel said.

Scratch's laughter once again filled the room. "Don't you, dear boy?"

Angel sighed. "There are factors that you seem to be discounting."

"I suppose you are referring to any so-called evidence you may have gleaned in last night's excursion to the North Pole. What did you get your hands on, Angel? What damning documentation have you dredged up that you believe could possibly damage my company?"

"We have the testimonies of elves you have wronged and video footage of the devastation you have wrought upon them. The squalid conditions, the lack of healthcare, the mass grave. You must know that we've already released it. It is already out there for the world to see."

"But will they believe it, dear boy?" Scratch asked. "Will they believe it?"

"The truth," Angel answered, "does not depend on whether one believes it. The truth is the truth."

Scratch chuckled. "You continue to surprise me, Angel. The truth is this. When presented with facts that are unsettling, most people prefer to believe in a comforting lie. Events of the last several years have proven that. The real truth is that believing in alternative, unsubstantiated *facts* is empowering. To claim without doubt that a lie is the truth both sets a person apart from the conforming crowd and binds them with others that profess to believe likewise. The lie makes them tribal. Powerful. It produces a kind of gleeful association. Believing in lies is a sort of alchemy—changing something, or someone, base into gold."

"I doubt that the world will look upon that mass grave growing daily on the edge of what was once Santa's village and not be repulsed," Angel said. "Your business depends on global goodwill and that, Mr. Scratch, your actions have destroyed."

"Oh tut, tut. I think that our contacts in the media can spot a deep fake when they see one." Scratch paused. "Especially if there is no one to step forward and corroborate its authenticity."

"You mean to kill us, then?" Angel asked.

"Kill? No. But you are obstacles that must be removed."

"The way you removed Claus the Second and Luther Deo?"

Scratch shrugged.

"Where are they?"

"Gone."

"Dead?"

"Not entirely."

"Then where?"

"Let's just say that there are places from which you cannot return." Scratch rose from his desk chair and motioned to his henchmen. "Now, Balthasar, would you kindly help our guests move forward. I'll need them closer to the desk."

"Of course," Balthasar answered, and he, Melchior and Caspar inched toward them.

"Stop!" the Claus shouted, stepping away from the wall. "This cannot be. There must be other ways to deal with these problems. I cannot allow—"

Scratch turned to train his eyes on the Claus. "*You* cannot allow?" he asked, his voice soft yet sinewy with menace. "Might I remind you that you work for me. You serve only at my pleasure. It would be a grave mistake for you to misconstrue the softheartedness that I have shown for you in the past for an unwillingness on my part to…" He paused. "To replace you."

"But the risk," the Claus insisted. "If, as Angel says, the video is out there, what will people think if those who supplied it abruptly vanish?"

"They will, I believe," Scratch said, "think whatever I tell them. They have in the past."

The Claus pointed to Angel. "But this no ordinary individual. How will his colleagues on the Archangelic Council react? Are you willing to risk their retribution?"

"Retribution, indeed," Scratch scoffed. "I confess that earlier this week when their leader, Michael, intervened on Mr. Angel's behalf, I briefly sought to enlist him as a buffer against any ill feelings they may have concerning our execution of Christmas. But I needn't have bothered. He rebuffed my offer, and in any case, I've come to realize that it was unnecessary. You've only to consider this. They cannot be unaware of what is transpiring here. Here, in this moment. And where are they, I ask you? Why haven't they interfered? I do not profess to understand their inky motives, but this I do know. The Archangelic Council and this poor unfortunate's former master allow all sorts of evil to run rife in the world. Do they stop it? As powerful as they profess to be, they surely could. But no. They stand aside, apart, watching, perhaps laughing at the pathetic condition of humanity. It's long puzzled me. I've long wondered what kind of a game they are playing." Scratch turned to Angel. "Perhaps you know. You were of their kindred. I ask you. What is their truth?"

"I don't claim to have all the answers either, Mr.

Scratch," Angel said. "But as Santa suggested, I think you are the one playing a dangerous game. Why take the risk? If you are so certain of the public's confidence in you, why not let us go? If you are correct, what harm can we do?"

"You are loose ends," Scratch said. "Unfinished business that I would I prefer be concluded before the holiday. We can't risk the kiddies' happiness come Christmas morning."

Scratch reached out to the lamp again, this time shining its beam on the large leather volume on his desk—on its intricate, hand-tooled design glowing there in the light. "Balthasar," he said, "would you kindly bring our guests forward."

Noel Baba broke his silence. "Might I offer a different perspective?" he asked. He shook himself slightly then adjusted the shirt sleeves that emerged from the cuffs of his dark suit. "I think you are looking at this in the wrong light, old man," he said. There was a confidence in his gaze and his voice was as loud and clear as if he were practicing for the stage. "I tend to agree that these individuals pose us no great harm. Particularly our Mrs. Deo." He smiled at his former employee. "Besides," he continued "we can't simply...disappear people."

"Of course, we can, Mr. Baba." There was ice in Scratch's voice. "As you well know. After all, I *disappeared* Mr. Bingle for you. Have you forgotten?"

Baba's smile froze, warping into a tremulous grin. "No, sir," he said.

"Well then," Scratch said and nodded once more at Balthasar.

Baba cast his eyes to Gloria Deo—eyes now awash

with fear and remorse. But there was no fear in her eyes. Angel saw in them only calm resolve. He couldn't have cared more for her than in that moment.

Scratch reached out and ran a flinger slowly, lovingly along the edge of the book on his desk. "Mr. Baba. Santa," he said. "You might want to step back."

As Scratch touched the book, Angel began to feel a mounting heaviness in his chest. He locked eyes with Scratch, then launched himself across the desk toward his old adversary. For an instant, alarm crackled in Scratch's eyes, but he had presence of mind enough to pivot out of the way and, as he did, he raised the book's cover.

Immediately Angel felt his trajectory change and he was jerked away from Scratch toward the open book. His vision blurred, his mind swirled, and the heaviness in his chest intensified. He felt as though his essence was collapsing on itself like that of a dying star—its core contracting, its light fading into darkness.

There was a humming sound growing ever louder. Angel didn't seem to be in the office any longer. Where he was now was brighter. Shards of light rotated around him. He too was whirling, tugged into a kind of vortex that had had opened before him, engulfing everything within its reach. But something was holding onto one of his legs helping him remain grounded. Angel planted his free leg hoping to resist the force that was drawing him slowly into oblivion. But his breathing was failing, and he soon realized that it was no use. He didn't have the strength. Perhaps he never had. This was the end. His final failure. Still, he struggled, thinking of poor Billy, his only friend. Of Gloria Deo. Her green eyes. Her radiant smile. Their relationship that never was and now would never be. Then his mind quieted. He took a last ragged breath and let go.

Angel landed heavily, painfully. Disoriented, he pushed himself to his knees, but when he tried to rise to his feet, he faltered and fell once again to the floor. He closed his eyes and groaned.

Hands gripped his arms. Angel felt himself being lifted. Somehow, he got his feet under him and, with help, stood weakly, wobbling in a room that still swirled.

Through the mist in his head, Angel heard Billy ask, "Are you okay, Boss?"

"Where am I? What happened?"

"You're with me, Boss," I've got you."

"But…"

The hands that had been supporting his arms left go and he had to take a couple of steps to keep his balance. As his vision cleared, he found that he was still in Scratch's office, Billy beside him. Angel did a slow survey of the room. The Claus and Fenster Dickens stood shoulder to shoulder staring at the now closed volume on the desk. Gloria Deo and Noel Baba were next to them. Baba had a protective hand on Mrs. Deo's elbow. Balthasar, Melchior, and Caspar had retreated near the door—nervous indecision crowding their features.

What was missing was Scratch.

"How did you…?" Angel began weakly. "Was it Michael? Did she…?"

"Oh, no. Harry," Billy told him. "It weren't her. You see what happened was, Scratch started to open that damned book and it was like we was all getting sucked into it. Sucked into the book." Billy shook his head incredulously. "I've never been so scared in my life. And you know that's saying something. You was closest, so you was going to get sucked in first. So, I grabbed your leg and held on for all I got. You were holding your own for a while, but it sure looked like you weren't gonna be with us long. None of us was. But then this here Baba guy jumps in and manages to pull Mrs. Deo into that corner there. Scratch started yelling and threatening. He was awful mad, Boss. Then it was the damnedest thing. Elvin gets into a crouch, puts his head down and drives a shoulder into the back of Scratch's legs. Looks like all of Elvin's time in the gym is paying off 'cause Scratch's knees buckled. He snarls one more time, but he tips headfirst toward the book, and he's gone. Just gone. The thing thuds shut and here we are."

Angel took in the scene—Billy beaming at the conclusion of his story, Baba holding tight to Mrs. Deo's arm, the Claus shaking his weary head, Dickens placing a consoling hand on his shoulder. And, their master gone, Balthasar and his goons standing uneasily by the office door. Balthasar took a deep breath, steadied himself, and slipped the gun he'd been holding into the pocket of his coat. Then he raised both eyebrows as though in salute and said, "Another time, Angel." He turned and the door, as though by telepathy, opened, allowing them into the hallway. But instead of making his exit, Balthasar let out a loud gasp and all three immediately backed into the office.

Michael stood in the hallway. She'd brought her sword this time. Fire burned in her eyes and her wings of pure white were spread wide in challenge. All three wise guys dropped to their knees before her. Trembling.

But Michael stepped past them, entered the office, and offered Angel a warm smile in greeting. For their part, Balthasar, Melchior, and Caspar quickly commando-crawled out into the hallway and made their escape.

Angel returned Michael's smile, but his was edged with uncertainty. "You're late," he said, his voice a mix of bewilderment and acceptance. "When I needed you most you didn't come for me."

Michael sheathed her sword, folded her wings, and stepped forward, placing a gentle hand against his cheek. "You didn't need me, Harry," she said. "You already had everything you needed."

Chapter Twenty-Nine

It was the day after Christmas, and it was obvious that Billy had been hitting the office bottle of Fingal's Cave heavily that morning. Angel regretted that he'd been unable to spend Christmas Day with his old friend. But since the encounter with Scratch, events had moved rapidly, calling Angel away from sharing the holiday with Billy as had long been their custom.

Billy sat slumped on the couch opposite Angel's desk, both hands wrapped around the half-empty bottle. When he heard Angel open the office door, Billy raised his head and managed an off-kilter smile. He peered at Angel, his eyes, red rimmed and bleary, went in and out of focus. After a moment, he said, "You're dressed funny, Boss. Where's your suit? I ain't seen you in nothing but a suit since…since…"

"Since I lost my wings," Angel finished for him.

Billy nodded, his head so heavy he nearly toppled ass over tea kettle. But he managed to right himself before tumbling to the floor. "That's right," Billy said. "What's that yer wearing?"

"It's a cloak," Angel told him.

"Very becoming," Billy slurred, then took a sip from the bottle. "That why I ain't seen you the last couple of days? You been hitting the menswear stores?"

Ignoring the sarcasm in his friend's voice, Angel entered the office, closing the door behind him. He was carrying a bag which he took behind the desk with him before sitting in his accustomed chair. He reached out a hand to the carriage clock, repositioned it slightly, looked up into his friend's eyes, and sighed. "I am sorry, Billy. You must know that I wanted to spend Christmas with you, but there was so much to do following Scratch's departure."

"You back with the Company? You working for Elvin now?" Billy hiccupped then closed his mouth tightly as if to ensure his stomach contents were not about to make an appearance. After a moment, he asked, "Heck, is Elvin even still in charge?"

"No. I am not working for the Company. And yes, for the time being, the current Claus remains in charge. He successfully dispatched his duties on Christmas Eve despite the recent upheaval and, it appears that in spite of the many compromises he's made thus far in his term as the Claus, he retains the confidence of those remaining at the Company." Angel paused. "Many top executives have quit. Most were informed that their services were no longer required, and their immediate departure would be their wisest course of action."

Billy chuckled. "With Scratch gone, Elvin's showing some balls, huh?"

Angel shrugged. "My guess is that, to a great degree, Santa is relying on the advice of Fenster Dickens. Most of the positions vacated by Scratch's human subordinates are being filled by elves. And now that Christmas is over, Santa is leading a delegation of both Company employees and the media to the Pole to fully document what has been happening up there. All of this has Dickens' stamp on it."

"He's a smart one, that Dickens," Billy said. "But

Scratch nearly had his number. Nearly had all of ours."

Billy pushed himself onto his feet and crossed to the desk, setting what was left of the scotch on its surface. Then he closed his eyes, gave himself a shake, and when he opened them, his vision seemed much less clouded.

"What about the broad?" he asked. "Gloria Deo. You two been seeing each other?"

Angel shook his head. "We talked. We agreed that it was best that our relationship remain cordial but distant. Especially since…" He stopped before he could finish the thought.

"Especially since what?" Billy pressed.

Angel reached into a desk drawer and drew out a shot glass. He filled it to the top with scotch and brought it carefully to his mouth, downing it in a single belt. "With her husband gone," Angel said, "Mrs. Deo has expressed a desire to return to her former profession. She's booked a singing engagement at The Night Visitor."

Billy leaned forward. "That mean she's back with Baba?"

Angel shook his head again. "I really don't know. But if she is, I believe that he will do his best to look out for her." He paused. "As always," he added.

"What's that, Boss?"

"Never mind."

Billy stared at Angel for a moment. "She's a strong woman," he said.

Angel smiled softly. "That she is."

Billy turned and made it most of the way back to the couch before he stopped suddenly and turned back to Angel. "And what about the book?" he asked. "What happens with the book?'

"That is currently in the hands of Fenster Dickens. But I suggested that he enlist the help of Dr. Richard Praetorius in examining it. Doc might be able to figure out how it works. Maybe even find a way to retrieve those entombed in it."

Billy gasped. "Wouldn't that mean Scratch could come back? How could—"

"Relax, Billy," Angel interrupted. "Just know that the book is in good hands and whatever happens with it will be done for the best."

"But they can't risk—"

"It isn't just Scratch that disappeared into it," Angel reminded him. "There's Claus the Second, Luther Deo, and we don't know how many others across how many centuries. The ethical thing to do is study the book with the goal of releasing those trapped in it if that is possible. Scratch is of secondary concern." He paused. "Especially since Scratch is hardly the only or even the most formidable emissary of the underworld."

"You mean—"

"I mean there is much evil in the universe. One can hardly deny that."

Billy nodded. "Oh, I know that, Boss."

Angel reached behind the desk for the bag he'd brought with him. "But let's not talk of that right now," he said, smiling. "Again, I'm sorry I missed Christmas, but I didn't forget to bring you a present."

An excited Billy clapped his hands together and eagerly stepped forward. "Oh, you didn't need to do that, Boss."

From the bag, Angel produced a box wrapped gaily in Christmas paper.

Taking it from Angel's hands, Billy tore at the paper

like a wolverine. Opening the box, he broke into a wide grin. Tipping the box so that Angel could see, Billy exclaimed, "It's just what I need! I mean, my old one is getting a bit ratty. I don't know if you noticed."

The box contained a brand-new line elf uniform complete with tunic, trousers, peaked hat, and pointy shoes—its colors bright as the northern lights on a clear night at the Pole.

"I noticed," Angel said. "So, you like it?"

"I love it. I mean—" Billy stopped suddenly, panic flashing in his eyes. "This doesn't mean…This doesn't mean that…" he stammered. "This doesn't mean I have to go back to work on the line, does it?"

Angel laughed. "No. Santa did mention that after all you've done to safeguard Christmas, a job would always be waiting for you at the Company. But, no, you are not being asked to go back to factory work."

Billy turned thoughtful. "Maybe some kind of cushy consultant job," he speculated. "You know, my own office. A secretary. Maybe my own major dumbo."

"I'll let you work that out with Santa."

"But, nah," Billy said, "that would mean I'd have to stop working for you."

"About that," Angel said.

Billy set the new uniform aside and stared at Angel, budding comprehension unfolding in his eyes. "There something you want to tell me, Boss?" He paused, then nodded at Angel.

"You gonna take off the cloak, Boss."

Angel stood, unfastened the clasp at the neck of the cloak, and let it fall to the floor. He took a deep breath before unfurling his bright white, thickly feathered wings.

Tears welled in Billy's eyes. "I'm happy for you, Boss. I really am." He paused. "This mean you're leaving?"

Angel nodded. "For a while at least. They are already talking assignments. Michael says it's about time I did some real work for a change."

Billy smiled and extended a hand to his friend. Angel shook it, then pulled Billy into a warm embrace.

"Don't worry about me, Boss," Billy said, his voice steady and strong. "I can take care of myself."

"I know. You always have. You've taken care of me, too."

The pair turned to look out the office window. Low gray clouds stretched wide to the horizon. But there was a lightening in the north offering the promise of sunshine.

Billy stepped back and smiled at Angel. "Well, if you ever need me again, you know where to find me. Right here in Yule Tide."

Angel reached down, picked up the cloak, draped it over his wings, and fastened it around his neck. Turning to the door, he said, "I'll be in touch."

Billy sniffed and stepped aside to watch his friend walk out of his life.

But before Angel was quite through the door, Billy stopped him, "Wait. I forgot to tell you."

Angel turned. "Tell me what?"

"Merry Christmas, Harry," Billy said.

Angel smiled. "Merry Christmas, Billy."

A word about the author...

Brian is the author of the Lyle Dahms mystery series. His novels spring from his lifelong love of mystery fiction, especially the works of Dashiell Hammett and Raymond Chandler, as well as more contemporary masters like Robert B. Parker and G.M. Ford. He is a three-time finalist in the Pacific Northwest Writers Association mystery and suspense contest and his first Dahms novel was a finalist in their Nancy Pearl Contest.

Yule Tide is his first standalone novel.

Brian spent much of his professional career working to alleviate domestic hunger serving as the operations director of the Emergency Feeding Program of Seattle & King County as well as the manager of the Pike Market Food Bank in downtown Seattle. Married with three beautiful daughters, Brian now lives and writes in Ocean Shores, a small city on the Washington coast. Visit him at www.brianandersonmysteries.com

Thank you for purchasing
this publication of The Wild Rose Press, Inc.

For questions or more information
contact us at
info@thewildrosepress.com.

The Wild Rose Press, Inc.
www.thewildrosepress.com